Betrayed

Ettie Smith Amish Mysteries Book 7

Samantha Price

Chapter 1

"Glen."

Elsa-May turned away from the pancakes she was cooking to look at her sister. "What did you say, Ettie?"

"I said 'Glen.' It's a man's name and I think it also means a forest or woodland."

Elsa-May's brow furrowed deeply as she continued to stare at her sister. "Who cares?"

"Anyone with the name of Glen would care."

"Why are you prattling on about the name 'Glen'? Do you know anyone by that name?"

"Nee."

Elsa-May huffed and turned back to the pancakes. "To be accurate, a glen is more of a ravine or a valley."

Breathing out her own huff of air, Ettie knew her sister was unable to refrain from correcting people so she let her words pass without comment. "What shall we do today?"

1

"Why don't you ask Glen what he's doing?"

"I don't know anybody called Glen, I just told you that."

Elsa-May chuckled. "What do you feel like doing?"

"I just want to get out of the *haus* and enjoy the sunshine. Should we go and visit someone? And don't say 'Glen.'"

"We could visit Ava and see what they've done with your old *haus.*"

"Why don't we go and visit someone we haven't seen in some time?"

Elsa-May flipped a pancake over. "This one's nearly ready. Well, hmm, let's see. We could go and visit Paula, the new woman."

"I suppose we could. I haven't seen her for a few weeks; I wonder if she's alright."

"We haven't heard that she's sick or anything." Elsa-May placed a pancake on a plate and handed it to Ettie.

"Denke, Elsa-May. This looks mighty good."

"Start now; don't wait for me." Elsa-May had

turned back toward the stove and hadn't noticed that Ettie had already poured syrup and started right in.

"Paula—didn't she have her *Englischer bruder* visiting her recently?"

"Jah. A couple of weeks ago; it could've been two or it could've been three. I haven't seen her since then."

Ettie said, "I do hope she is okay. Surely other people would've checked on her."

"I don't know why we didn't think to visit her sooner. She could be lying in bed sick."

"Or maybe she's left us already," Ettie suggested.

"Surely not. She's been in the community about nine months now, or is it longer than that?"

"It must be nearly a year now."

"Remember Sheila Hanks and her *familye?*" Elsa-May asked.

"Jah. They were in the community for a year and then left just as suddenly as they had arrived."

"Not everyone's the same, Ettie. I'm just saying that you can't tell. We'll visit her, but you'll have to wait until I take Snowy for a walk."

"Haven't you done that already?" Ettie asked.

Elsa-May frowned. "I woke up and came straight out here, and made the breakfast. When exactly do you think I would've found the time? I normally go right after I eat."

"I was only asking a question."

"It won't take long. You can come with us."

Ettie scoffed at the idea. "This is the only peace I get from you two all day. I thought I'd missed my break today, but now I'll be awake to enjoy it. Off you go."

"How about I eat my pancakes first? Is that alright with you?" Elsa-May loaded pancake on her fork.

Ettie giggled. "If you must. I'll clean the dishes while you're walking the dog and then we can leave right away."

"Snowy! Not 'the dog.'"

Ettie rolled her eyes. "Okay 'Snowy'—who just happens to be a dog."

Elsa-May and Snowy had been gone for fifteen minutes and Ettie had just finished straightening up the kitchen when a knock sounded on the front door. *Silly old girl locked the door on herself.* "Why did you lock…" Ettie opened the door, but instead of Elsa-May and Snowy, it was Detective Kelly. "Oh, it's you!"

"Nice to see you too, Mrs. Smith."

"I was expecting Elsa-May."

"Does she usually knock on her own door, or did you two have another spat and you locked her out?"

"Not at all. She's walking Snowy, and when I heard the knock I thought she'd locked herself out."

"Ah, yes, I just passed her and the dog down the road."

"You mustn't call him 'the dog' in front of Elsa-May—it's Snowy." Ettie chuckled, but when the detective's face didn't crack a smile, she cleared her throat. "You'd better come in. I take it this isn't a social visit?"

"I'm afraid it's not."

"Come in and sit down."

"Thank you." When he'd sat down, he continued, "Something's happened. There's been a brutal attack on a young Amish woman. That's why I'm here."

"Who? Not Paula Peters?"

The detective's eyebrows flew upward. "How did you know?"

"It's Paula?"

"Yes!"

A breathless Elsa-May hurried through the door with Snowy, and Ettie and Detective Kelly turned to look at her.

"Detective Kelly, I saw your car. What is it? Is anything wrong?"

Ettie spoke before the detective could. "Quick come in and sit down. You'll never believe what Detective Kelly just told me. There's been a death and we were just talking about the person only moments ago."

Elsa-May gasped and covered her mouth. "Not

Glen?"

"Of course not Glen! We've established that we don't know anybody called Glen."

Not wanting to be wrong, Elsa-May added, "Well, we *were* just talking about him."

"And the fact that he doesn't exist."

Detective Kelly frowned and looked between the two of them.

Elsa-May said, "You're just trying to make me look silly in front of the detective."

"I wouldn't do that! I don't know what you're talking about."

Detective Kelly raised his hand in the air. "Is it too early to drink?"

"Not at all. I'll make you a nice cup of hot tea." Ettie pushed herself to her feet.

"Don't trouble yourself. That's not the drink I was thinking of."

Ettie sat back down. "Put the dog outside, Elsa-May, and when you're sitting down I'll tell you what's just happened."

"The young woman's not dead, Ettie."

"She's not? I thought you said she was."

"Who are we talking about?" Elsa-May asked, still standing there. "Wait! I'll put Snowy outside." When Elsa-May returned, she sat down and stared at Kelly. "Okay, continue."

"I was just telling Ettie that Paula Peters, a woman from your community was brutally attacked and left for dead."

"We were just going to visit her today," Elsa-May said.

"She's not dead?" Ettie asked Kelly.

"No, she was brutally attacked is what I said, I never told you she was dead. And I'm afraid, Elsa-May, she won't be getting any visitors for some time. She's in the hospital in critical condition and may not pull through."

"That's dreadful. What happened?" Ettie asked.

"We know what happened but we don't know who. That's why I'm here.

I need your help once more, Mrs. Smith."

"Okay, I'll help if I can."

"What do you know about Ms. Peters?" he asked.

"She's only been in our community for at most twelve months. I don't know much about her past before she joined us. All I heard is that her family is wealthy and they were dreadfully upset that she came to us. I know she has a brother because I heard he had visited her recently. When she first came to join our community, the bishop placed her with the Lapp family."

"Yes," Elsa-May joined in, "she stayed with the Lapps for three months and then she bought her own place."

"She's single?"

"Yes, single."

"We thought from her house that she was, since there was no evidence of anyone else living there. I haven't spoken to the neighbors yet. I came here as soon as I could. I've got officers interviewing everyone in the street to see if anyone saw or heard anything."

"She probably wouldn't have remained single for long because there were a few men interested in her, I'm certain. She's a looker."

"Ettie means she's an attractive young woman."

"Yes, I gathered that. I'll need the names of any young men who were keeping company with her; also anyone who took an interest in her. She would've formed some close relationships within the community I assume?"

Ettie nodded. "We'll see what we can find out."

"Did she work?" Kelly asked.

Ettie opened her mouth to reply.

The detective said, "No; don't tell me now. Can you come down to the station this afternoon? I'll have more information by then and we can work out how best to approach things. I've got the evidence technicians at Paula's house right now."

"Ettie and I were going out today, so we'd be happy to stop by the station later in the day."

"Good." The detective rose to his feet.

"Can't we visit Paula in the hospital?" Elsa-May asked.

"She's unconscious and in critical condition. We've got an officer stationed by her door. There are strictly no visitors allowed until she regains

10

consciousness. And she'll have to speak with me before anyone else."

"Not even the bishop? Can't he visit?"

"No, Ettie." He scratched his head. "We'll see what we can arrange. Come to think of it, you could give me the bishop's address. He might be able to help me with a number or address for her family."

"Yes, of course. I'll write it out for you."

While Ettie was writing the address out, Elsa-May walked him toward the door. "Do you have any idea at all who might have done this?" Elsa-May asked.

"We found some evidence, but it won't mean anything until we find out whose it is."

"That sounds intriguing. What kind of evidence?"

"A piece of jewelry, a locket on a chain, that must've been pulled off in the struggle."

"Struggle?" Elsa-May asked.

"Poor Paula. I hope she'll be okay." Ettie joined them and handed the address of the bishop to Detective Kelly.

"You could pray for her," Kelly said quietly.

"The news I've heard is that she might not pull through."

"We'll be praying for her," Elsa-May said.

"We'll see you later this afternoon, Detective."

He nodded. "Yes, I'll see you then."

Elsa-May closed the door and turned to Ettie. "He seemed distracted."

"He's probably just upset. It must be hard to be faced with tragedy and upheaval every day."

Ettie nodded. "I keep telling him he needs to take a break. He works far too hard."

"What's your plan for today?"

"Why don't we stop by Paula's *haus?*"

"Okay, but Kelly said there were forensic people all over her home. They'll have taped it off and we won't be allowed near it."

Ettie pushed her lips together. "I think we need to start there. Even if we can't get in."

Elsa-May shrugged. "Okay, if that's what you want to do."

"I wonder who would want to hurt her."

"Could she have been escaping a dark past? Is

that why she joined our community?"

"You could be right."

"We need to talk with the people who knew her before she came here, as well as the new friends she's made."

"We've got a big day ahead of us."

Chapter 2

"Did Detective Kelly say there was a locket found?" Ettie asked Elsa-May.

"Jah, a locket, which is jewelry. Women wear lockets with the photo, or the hair, of a loved one inside."

"I know what a locket is, Elsa-May. So the detective must think a woman attacked her?"

"Yes, unless it was Paula's keepsake and got ripped off her neck in the struggle."

"She wouldn't have brought anything with her like that from her old life. She would've had to put her old life behind her."

Elsa-May leaned forward. "She might have, except for the locket."

"It'll be easy enough for the detective to find out who owns it if there's a photo inside the locket."

"That's true. I do hope Paula will be okay."

"We didn't even ask Kelly how she was found—I mean, who found her. She lives alone. I wonder if someone visited her just like we were going to visit her today."

"That's one of the questions we can ask when we see him this afternoon."

"Come on, Ettie, let's go."

"I'm ready." The two women hurried down the road to the shanty that housed the telephone used by the residents on their street, and Ettie called for a taxi.

While they waited for the taxi, Elsa-May said, "Are you sure we should go to Paula's *haus?*"

Ettie nodded emphatically.

"They'll have tape across the place and the forensic people might still be in there looking for things. You know how long they take. They'll be there all day and half the night."

"You already mentioned the tape business, but I feel we should start there. Even if we can't get in, there might be people hanging around—like neighbors we can talk with."

"I guess that's as good a place as any to start."

The taxi pulled up at Paula's house, and it was

just as the sisters had expected. There was yellow crime scene tape criss-crossed in front of the house, along with a string of police cars parked outside.

"You can drop us here," Ettie said to the taxi driver.

When they'd paid the driver, they walked out to join a crowd of people who had gathered to watch what the police were doing.

They noticed Elizabeth Esh outside the house next door. Elizabeth waved to them.

With her elbow, Ettie jabbed Elsa-May in her side. "Let's go over and ask Elizabeth if she saw anything."

Ettie scurried off and Elsa-May did her best to keep up with her.

"Hello, have you heard?" Elizabeth asked the sisters when they walked through her front gate.

"*Jah,* we heard; that's why we're here." Elsa-May joined Elizabeth just outside her front door and Ettie wasn't far behind her.

"Did you see or hear what happened, Elizabeth?" Ettie asked.

"I was the one who called the police and the ambulance."

"Did you see who did this to her?" Ettie asked.

"I saw her. She stepped out of the *haus* and then collapsed on the ground. I ran to her and I thought she was dead. She had passed out, so I ran back to Mr Grayson's *haus* and asked him to call 911."

Ettie knew that Mr Grayson lived a few doors down.

"Are you all right, Elizabeth?" Elsa-May asked.

"I am, but I feel a bit shaky."

"How about Elsa-May and I make you a cup of hot tea?"

Elizabeth nodded. "That sounds like a good idea. Let's all go inside and have some tea."

When they were seated with tea in front of them, Elizabeth told them what she knew. "It was in the early hours of the morning. I had just woken up and I was putting the pot on to boil in the kitchen like I usually do, and I just happened to look outside and I saw her. I have a clear view of the front of her *haus* from my kitchen window."

"Did you see anyone before that, or hear any cars?" Ettie asked before she took a mouthful of tea.

"I heard nothing at all and I saw nothing. Have you heard how she is?"

"She's in critical condition. The detective we talked with this morning said she might not make it."

"We must pray for her."

"Jah, we will keep praying. After we spoke to the detective this morning, he was going to the bishop's *haus* to see if he could find details of any of Paula's relatives or friends."

"Would you happen to know of any?" Elsa-May asked Elizabeth.

"Or did she still keep company with *Englischers?"* Ettie asked.

"I don't know her that well. I see her to wave to every day, and she pops over for a cup of tea every now and again. I've never asked her about her past. The old things are passed away, and all things have become new. Why talk about the past when it's dead and buried?"

The sisters murmured in agreement.

"So you're helping the police again, Ettie?" Elizabeth asked.

"The detective asked me to help him. He has the problem that no one in the community will speak with him."

"There's not much difference talking with him or talking to you, is there? If you are just going to repeat everything to him that people tell you."

"I don't see it that way," Ettie said.

"We're only trying to help people, Elizabeth. It's not as though we get people into trouble by helping the detective. So far the outcomes have been helpful to the community, and many times Ettie's helped keep community members out of jail when they've been falsely accused."

"Well, not just me, Elsa-May. I've only played a small part," Ettie said. "Other people have helped."

"Of course you'd see things that way, Elsa-May," Elizabeth said. "You're like an informant, Ettie."

Ettie pulled her mouth to one side, not liking

what her friend said.

Elizabeth continued, "Everyone in the community knows you're friendly with that detective fellow. What's his name—Crawly?"

"Crowley, and he's retired. The current one is Detective Kelly." Ettie figured it was time to go and she gave her sister a nod.

Elsa-May drained her teacup. "It was a good thing you saw Paula when you did. From the sounds of it, she might not have survived if you hadn't been so quick to call 911."

"*Gott* was watching over her," Elizabeth responded.

"*Denke* for the tea, Elizabeth, but we've got a bit to do today, so we better get going."

"What are you going to do today?" Elizabeth asked.

"We've got a few errands to run," Elsa-May said.

"Did you know any of Paula's friends or family?" Ettie thought she might as well ask once again. "I heard that she had her *bruder* visit her recently."

"There's always a man coming to visit her, and

he's an *Englischer.* I didn't take too much notice. He could be her *bruder.* Why do you ask?"

Ettie didn't want to say that she was asking to help the detective out. She didn't want another lecture from Elizabeth. "I'm just wondering who might have done this to her."

"It's not our business, is it, Ettie, to go poking around in people's lives?"

"If you hadn't interfered in Paula's life she might not be alive today," Elsa-May said. "You poked around in her life by calling 911. Let's put things into perspective."

"I never poked around in anyone's life. I was helping Paula by calling the paramedics."

"You called 911. That's kind of like poking around in someone's life; you didn't just leave her there to die."

"That's two very different things, Elsa-May." Elizabeth rose to her feet and Ettie and Elsa-May knew they had worn out their welcome.

"Thank you for the tea, Elizabeth," Ettie said.

"You're welcome."

Ettie and Elsa-May picked up their tea cups.

"Just leave them there. I'll clear up," Elizabeth said.

When they were outside in the street, Ettie turned to her sister. "She wasn't any help whatsoever."

"*Nee!* She seemed annoyed with you, Ettie. What did you do to upset her?"

"I don't know if I've done anything to upset the woman." Ettie looked over at the small crowd of onlookers still outside Paula's house. "Let's see what we can overhear. If we just stand amongst them, we might be able to hear something useful."

"It's worth a try I suppose."

As soon as they approached the crowd, everyone started moving away.

"There's nothing to see here ladies," a police officer said as he walked over near them.

Ettie looked up at him. "We know the woman who lives here. She's a friend of ours."

"Is that so? We might need to speak with you, then." He pulled out a pad and a pen from his shirt pocket. "What's your name?"

Elsa-May responded, "We've already got an appointment to see Detective Kelly later this afternoon."

He closed his notepad and put it back into his pocket along with his pen. "Very good."

"What happened here?" Ettie asked.

"I can tell you the same thing Detective Kelly will tell you this afternoon. Someone wanted your friend dead." The man turned to walk away.

Ettie took a step toward him. "Did the technicians find any evidence?"

He turned back, and smiled at her. "I can't tell you that, I'm sorry, Mrs?"

"Mrs. Smith."

"I can't tell you that, Mrs. Smith."

"And you are?"

"Senior Constable Barker." He gave her and Elsa-May a nod, and then walked to a police car and got in the passenger seat.

"You weren't exactly subtle, Ettie."

"I stopped being subtle ten years ago."

Elsa-May chuckled. "Where will we go now?"

"I'm not certain. No one's being very helpful."

"Well you're the person who usually knows what's going on in the community, Ettie, and if you don't know very much about this woman who would? Who is she friends with?"

"The Lapps would probably know her best, but I don't want to be the one to tell them someone attacked Paula and put her in the hospital."

"It's not as though she's dead."

"I suppose you're right. Let's go visit the Lapps, then." Ettie walked off.

"Ettie, where are you going? There's a public phone back this way to call for the taxi." When Ettie didn't answer her, Elsa-May hurried to catch up with her.

Ettie rapped on the window of the police car causing Senior Constable Barker to roll down the window. "Would you be going back to the police station now? When you leave here?"

"Yes. Do you want us to take you to speak with Detective Kelly now?"

Ettie screwed up her nose. "He said he wanted

to see us later in the afternoon and he'll get cranky if we turn up any earlier. I was wondering if you would take us somewhere else. It's on the way."

He smiled. "Cranky, eh? Can't have that. Certainly, we can give you a ride. My partner will only be two minutes." He got out and opened the back door for them.

Once they were seated in the car, Ettie gave Elsa-May a huge smile, leaned in and whispered, "It beats paying for a taxi."

Elsa-May smiled. "I have to agree with that."

The officer got back into the front passenger seat. "So you knew this lady well?" he asked them.

"She's relatively new to our community, but we had gotten to know her reasonably well."

"That's why the detective wants to talk to us; to see if we can help him in any way," Elsa-May added.

Another officer got into the driver's seat and turned around to look at the elderly ladies.

Senior Constable Barker laughed. "We've got a couple of passengers."

"I can see that, but where are we taking them?" the officer asked.

Ettie leaned forward. "It's on the way. We need to visit someone to help with the information we're to give Detective Kelly later today. Just start driving back to your police station and I'll let you know when we get closer."

"Yes, Ma'am." The officer started the engine. "But don't ask me to put the siren on."

Ettie and Elsa-May giggled like a couple of girls.

After the sisters had been dropped off at the end of the long driveway at the Lapps' property, they began the trek up the driveway.

"This is such a long walk. I never realized this before."

"When was the last time we visited them?" Ettie asked.

"It would be some time. We didn't bring anything with us."

"There's nothing we can do about that now. We couldn't ask the police to drive us to a bakery and bring us back here."

"I hope you're going to do all the talking, Ettie."

"If you let me I will. You tend to interrupt me at the very worst times."

"*Nee.* You usually do that to me."

Ettie gritted her teeth. "I'll talk and you can fill in things that I leave out."

"I suppose we'll have to tell them what happened to her, first off," Elsa-May said.

"We, or me?" Ettie asked.

"You. I'll keep quiet. I hope Paula's okay."

"Yes, I do, too. Don't forget the main reason we're here is to find out who Paula was friendly with. We'll most likely have to find the people they mention, whether they are friends or *familye.*"

"Got it."

When they reached the house, there was no sign of anyone about.

"Knock on the door and see if anyone's home," Elsa-May ordered.

Ettie knocked on the door and waited a while. When no one answered, she pushed the door open. "Hello! Hello, is anyone home?"

Elsa-May passed Ettie and walked into the living room. Ettie followed. They stood still and looked around.

"There's no one home," Elsa-May said.

"What do we do now?"

"I suppose we'll have to think of someone else to ask about Paula."

Ettie suggested, "We'll call for a taxi and then while we're waiting for it, we'll figure out what to do next."

They closed the door and headed to the barn where they knew the Lapps' had their phone.

When they pushed the door of the barn open, the interior was so dark that they could barely see.

"Push the other door open, Ettie."

"What? The other door?"

"Jah."

Just as Ettie pushed the second of the side-by-side barn doors open, a deep voice boomed from somewhere within the barn. "Who's there?"

Ettie and Elsa-May jumped.

"It's Ettie and Elsa-May," Ettie said.

"Who is it?" the monotone voice asked again.

Ettie knew it was the Lapp's nineteen-year-old son, Obadiah. "Obadiah, it's Ettie Smith and Elsa-May Lutz."

Obadiah stepped into the shaft of light coming in through the doors and lighting the darkness of the barn. He was a simple boy and they knew he had various learning difficulties.

"Obadiah! You gave us quite a fright," Elsa-May said.

"We were looking for your *mudder* and *vadder*. Do you know where they are?"

"They're at the hospital. My girlfriend is in the hospital."

"Your girlfriend?" Ettie asked.

Elsa-May took a step toward him. "You mean Paula?"

"Yep!"

"Paula is your girlfriend?" Ettie asked, amazed. It was possible, she realized, that Paula knew nothing of this.

"Yep."

Elsa-May asked, "How did your parents know Paula was in the hospital?"

"Someone hit her. On her head." He rapped his knuckles on his head.

"*Jah,* we heard about that and that's dreadful news, but who told them about Paula?"

"I got a phone call."

"Who called you?"

He shook his head. "Dunno."

"Is it okay if we use the phone to call a taxi?" Ettie asked.

He nodded and continued to stare at them, as Ettie pulled Elsa-May's sleeve so she'd go with her to the corner of the barn where the phone was.

Chapter 3

Ettie and Elsa-May filled in time around town, and before they knew it, it was late afternoon. They made their way to the station to see Detective Kelly.

When the sisters were seated in front of the detective, Elsa-May asked, "How is Paula?"

"Her condition remains unchanged." He breathed out heavily and placed his elbows on his desk. "Did you manage to find out anything for me?"

"We talked to the neighbor, Elizabeth, but she didn't tell us much."

"She's the one who called 911?" Kelly asked.

Ettie and Elsa-May nodded.

"That is disappointing."

"Yes, it is," Ettie had to agree.

"I thought you of all people would be able to get information from her, Ettie."

"She seemed rather hostile for some reason."

"Elizabeth told us that Paula had a man who

often visited her, but I guess she'd already told you that," Elsa-May said.

"It was the fellow on the other side who told my officers about the frequent visitor, Mr… something starting with G, I think, if I can trust my memory." He rustled through his paperwork. "I'll find it later."

Ettie said, "There's Mr. Grayson who lives a few doors down from our friend, Elizabeth, but I don't know the man who lives directly on the other side of Paula. Elizabeth called 911 from Mr. Grayson's phone."

"No, it wasn't a Mr. Grayson. It's in my paperwork—somewhere." He looked back up at the sisters. "Can you go back and speak with Elizabeth some more tomorrow?"

"Why?" Elsa-May asked.

"Sometimes when people have time to cool down and think about things they can rethink their reluctance to speak. I'm certain she knows more than she's said. Otherwise, she wouldn't have been so uncooperative."

"I don't see that it will do any good," Ettie said, trying to work out what Detective Kelly meant by his last comment. It didn't make sense.

Elsa-May leaned forward. "What did your team find out from the evidence?"

"Firstly, there are the fingerprints on the tire iron, which was obviously the murder weapon that was left behind. The locket we found suggests a female perpetrator, and then there was the information we got from the non-Amish man living on the other side of Paula."

"And what did he say?" Elsa-May asked.

"Detective Kelly just told us that," Ettie said.

"It's okay, Ettie, it's a lot to take in." Kelly turned to Elsa-May. "He was the one who told us that Paula had a regular male visitor. You already know what happened when we questioned Elizabeth." He chuckled.

Elsa-May puffed out her cheeks. "I'm glad it wasn't only us she didn't want to speak with."

"You mentioned that Paula couldn't have any visitors in the hospital, but when we went to visit the Lapps, their youngest son told us that his parents were at the hospital visiting her."

"She's had no visitors. They might have tried to see her, but they wouldn't have had any luck. You say their son told you?"

"That's right, and he thinks he's Paula's boyfriend." Ettie giggled.

The detective leaned forward and clasped his hands on the desk in front of him. "Is that so?"

Ettie frowned, not liking the way the detective was appearing interested in the boy. "Yes, but you said yourself it was a female perpetrator."

"At this stage, it looks that way, but it's early days yet." The detective leaned back in the chair. "What did you say his name was?"

"Ettie didn't say what his name was."

Ettie frowned at Elsa-May. There was no point getting on the wrong side of the detective. "His name is Obadiah Lapp."

Elsa-May added, "Don't go thinking Obadiah would be Paula's boyfriend. It would all be in his mind. He's a simple boy with the mind of a ten-year-old."

"According to my officers, Paula had a regular male visitor."

"An Amish one?" Ettie asked.

"No, but an Amish man could've dressed in other clothes if he'd had ill intent."

"That's not likely. Paula would wonder why the man would be dressing like an *Englischer*. If you're suspicious of Obadiah, you should know that he'd be too simple to think of being devious. And when I say simple, I'm not being rude about him; it's just the best way I can think of to describe him."

"I know you wouldn't be rude about anybody," the detective said.

Ettie noticed that the detective wrote down Obadiah's name.

"He's a teenager?" he asked.

Elsa-May nodded. "Yes."

"And the Lapps are the people that Paula stayed with when she first joined your community?" he asked.

"That's right."

"But he's not guilty of anything," Ettie said.

"Well, that's what I aim to find out when I question him later today."

Ettie and Elsa-May turned slightly to face each other. They didn't like the sound of that.

"Did you find out anything from the bishop about Paula's *familye?*" Ettie asked.

"Your bishop was kind enough to give us the address he had for the family—her parents to be exact. I sent two of my best officers out there. They told me her family was extremely distressed about Paula being in the hospital. And they were distressed about her joining a cult. They said it wouldn't have happened if she hadn't joined."

"We're not a cult," Elsa-May said with a huff.

Ettie nearly choked.

He picked up his pen and went on without comment. "Now back to Obadiah Lapp. What does he look like? Tall, dark hair, with a solid build?"

"Yes that's right."

"Interesting. He matches the description of the man who was visiting Paula."

"Didn't you say that he was an *Englischer*—the man who was visiting her?" Ettie said to drive her point home again.

Elsa-May added, "Did he visit her in a buggy or a car?"

"I hear what you're saying, and I know you don't like it, but I'm going to question him anyway."

"You'll be wasting your time, but if that's what you want to do, go right ahead."

"Mrs. Smith, I hardly need your permission to question anybody that I see fit."

Ettie lifted up her chin and pressed her lips together.

Elsa-May said, "Ettie's just concerned that you're wasting your time when there's someone still out there who tried to harm Paula."

"I wouldn't be doing my job properly if I didn't bring the fellow in for questioning." He looked at Ettie. "Mrs. Smith, I would really like you to go back and talk to the neighbour. I have faith in you that you'll be able to get some information out of her. Elizabeth must've seen comings and goings.

39

She wouldn't talk to my officers—just grunted at them."

"I don't think it will do any good."

"Just do it, please, Mrs. Smith. You might be surprised what she's remembered when she's had some time to think things through and let her emotions settle."

Ettie nodded. "I'll do it. Can you tell me what else you've found out?"

Detective Kelly breathed out heavily, picked up the folder on his desk, and opened it. "Let me see what remains to tell you. I've covered the necklace that was found…"

"The locket. Yes."

The detective looked up at Elsa-May and frowned, obviously not liking to be interrupted. "We were lucky enough to find a man's photograph in that locket, which might prove useful. We've got fingerprints on what appears to be the assault weapon. Then we've got the male visitor." He closed the folder. "The best thing we can hope for is that Paula regains consciousness and tells us exactly what happened."

Ettie nodded. "How long do the fingerprint results take to come back?"

"They can take up to two days, and if the prints aren't in the system, they won't lead us to an ID."

"We know that much," Elsa-May said.

He stared at Elsa-May, and then said to Ettie, "Are you going back to talk to Elizabeth today?"

"No," Elsa-May answered for Ettie.

Ettie finally said, "Tomorrow. It's too late today."

"We'll go first thing tomorrow after breakfast." Elsa-May gave a nod.

"Very good. I appreciate that." The detective took another look at the list and frowned.

Elsa-May asked, "Can't read your own writing?"

Detective Kelly laughed. "It's like that sometimes. I was in a hurry when I wrote this."

"Before we go, let me get this straight for Elsa-May's sake," Ettie said. "You've got fingerprints on the weapon, a locket, a man's photograph is in the locket, and a man seen visiting Paula?" Ettie didn't look Elsa-May's way because she knew her sister was scowling at her.

"That's correct." He rustled through the papers again and then picked up one of the pages. "The male neighbor on the opposite, Mr. Duggor—I was wrong it didn't start with a G—didn't hear anything that night, and your friend, Elizabeth, didn't hear anything. According to what Elizabeth told the paramedics, she saw Paula staggering out of the house in the early hours of the morning, and then Paula collapsed outside the front door. The next couple of days should prove interesting, when the forensic results begin to come back."

"I hope so," Ettie said.

Chapter 4

The next morning, Ettie and Elsa-May made their way back to Elizabeth's house only because Ettie had told Detective Kelly she would.

On the way there in the taxi, Ettie said, "We should try a new approach since the old one didn't work."

"Cake is an icebreaker."

Ettie giggled. "Do you think so?"

Elsa-May nodded.

"What about cake *and* flowers?"

"That would be going too far."

With a shrug of her shoulders, Ettie said, "If you say so. Just the cake would work for me."

"Right; very good. No flowers it is, then."

"I'm glad we've established that."

Elsa-May leaned over to the driver and directed him to the nearest cake shop. The driver and Ettie waited in the car while Elsa-May chose a cake. When she got back in the car, she passed the cake box to Ettie, and then waved a bag of hard caramels.

"Candy! Excellent idea."

"Are you ladies done with the detours?" the taxi driver asked.

"Yes. You can take us to the address we gave you now."

When Paula's house came into view, the taxi driver commented, "I've never been to this part of town in my five years of working this area, and now this is the second time in as many days I've been to this very street."

"Really?" Elsa-May commented.

"Which house did you go to?" Ettie asked.

"She just wanted to be let out at the end of the street."

Elsa-May lunged forward. "Do you remember what she looked like?"

He shook his head. "Can't say that I do. It was at night."

"Old or young?"

"Middling to youngish. She wasn't a teenager. I'd say in her thirties if I had to guess."

Elsa-May handed the driver money and he gave her back some change.

"Where did you collect the lady from?" Elsa-May inquired further.

He frowned. "In town somewhere."

"Could I borrow a pen for a quick moment? I won't hold you up for too long."

The driver handed Ettie a pen.

"Elsa-May, give me that receipt you got for the cake."

When Elsa-May passed the receipt over, Ettie scratched down the driver's name and ID number that were clearly displayed on the dashboard. "Thank you." She handed back the pen and tucked the receipt into her sleeve.

"You wrote his ID down?" Elsa-May asked when they'd gotten out of the car.

"It was strange that the woman had him drop her at the end of the street and not at a particular house, don't you think."

"*Jah,* it is odd. Are you going to give his details to the detective?"

"Of course I am. The driver would surely keep some kind of a logbook, or the people who make the bookings for him must have some kind of records."

When Elizabeth opened the door, she smiled when her eyes settled on the cake box that Ettie held out toward her.

"What's this?"

"It's a lemon sponge cake."

"And we thought you might like some hard caramel candy," Elsa-May said.

"Wunderbaar, denke. I love any kind of candy, and lemon cake is a particular favorite." As Elizabeth stood aside to let them in, Elsa-May glanced at Ettie and gave her a look as if to say, 'I told you so.'

"Come to the kitchen and I'll boil the teakettle. It's just been boiled not long ago, so it shouldn't take long. Tea for you two?"

"Jah, please," Ettie said, sitting in the chair next to her sister who'd already taken a seat.

"Tea for you two, plus me, makes tea for three."

Elizabeth gave a little laugh as she lit the gas burner beneath the teakettle. Then she opened the box and looked in at the cake. "Lovely." She took a knife and sliced into the cake. "What brings the two of you back here today? I told you all I know yesterday."

Ettie was glad that Elizabeth seemed in a much better frame of mind. "We got to thinking that you must know some of the goings on next-door. More than you told us yesterday. We've heard that she often had a tall dark handsome man visit her—an *Englischer.*"

"Oh Ettie! There was no mention of him being handsome," Elsa-May said.

"Tall, dark, with a solid build—he'd *have* to be handsome too."

Elsa-May shook her head. "You people! Tall dark men aren't necessarily handsome."

Ettie's lips turned down at the corners and she looked up at Elizabeth. "What would you think, Elizabeth? Are most tall dark men handsome as well?"

"Let me think about that for a minute." Elizabeth placed the cake in the middle of the table along with the cake server. Then she placed three small plates on the table. "Help yourselves to the cake." When she pushed the cake toward them, she said, "I agree with Ettie. Tall and dark goes along with being handsome." Elizabeth laughed and sat down at the table with them.

"See, Elsa-May? Two against one."

Elsa-May shook her head again. "It doesn't bother me whether he was handsome or not. Why are you making such a big fuss about it, Ettie?"

"*Jah,* what's this about the man, Ettie?" Elizabeth asked.

Elizabeth had perked up and was friendlier than she'd been the day before. Whether it was the talk of handsome men or the lemon sponge cake, Ettie didn't know.

"I was just saying that a tall dark man was often seen visiting Paula. Do you know whether that was a friend or maybe her *bruder?*"

Elizabeth had just popped a portion of cake into

48

her mouth, so she had to wait until she swallowed before she answered the question. "I'd seen that man visiting her every few days. It's not my place to mention that to the bishop or anybody else. I'm not Paula's keeper."

Elsa-May interrupted Elizabeth, "So you thought it possible that there was funny business going on?"

"I couldn't really say. I wasn't going to mention anything and look like a fool if there was a good reason for the man to be at her *haus*. I'd look silly, not to mention that I'd ruin a neighborly friendship with Paula. You just said it could've been her *bruder*. I'm not an interfering person. Paula keeps to herself and so do I."

"I see."

"So you didn't see if the man was handsome?" Elsa-May's eyes twinkled.

"I thought you didn't care about handsome," Ettie said.

Elizabeth answered before Elsa-May could, "It's possible that he was. I got the number of his car, if that's any good to you."

Elsa-May's mouth fell open.

"You really took down the plate number of his car?" Ettie asked.

"*Jah,* I did. I thought it wouldn't hurt to know who was visiting her. I'm not certain why I took it down, but now I'm glad I did."

Elsa-May frowned. "Why are you only mentioning this now?"

"I didn't think of it before," Elizabeth said.

"Can you give it to us?"

"*Jah,* of course. I'll find it. I'm sure I put it somewhere; oh yes, it's in the drawer of my small writing desk."

"Were you suspicious of the man or something to take his plate number down?" Ettie asked.

Elsa-May leaned toward Elizabeth. "She means, what made you write it down?"

Ettie turned to her sister and narrowed her eyes.

"You can never be too careful." Elizabeth stood up when the hot water bubbled loudly. "Now, do you have milk and sugar in your tea?"

"We both have it weak and black," Ettie said.

"We used to have cream, but with Elsa-May having to lose weight we've both cut down on small things like cream in our tea."

"Oh Ettie, Elizabeth doesn't need to know about all of that."

"That's all right. I found it interesting, and quite pleasing because I don't have any cream in the *haus.*" Elizabeth gave a small laugh and then poured the tea and sat down once she'd given each sister a cup.

"Denke for being so helpful, Elizabeth," Ettie said. "We just want to find out who attacked Paula so awfully."

"I went to the hospital after you two left me yesterday. They wouldn't let me see her. Have you heard how she is today?"

"Nee we haven't. I hope she's all right. The detective told us that she had a police officer right outside her door and no one was allowed to see her, not even her own *familye.* We haven't even tried to visit her because we know we wouldn't get in," Ettie said.

"Jah, it was the policeman who said I couldn't go in. He was very insistent about it. I explained that I lived right next door to her, but it made no difference to him."

Elsa-May nodded. "I do hope the poor girl will recover properly and not have any complications from the attack."

"So, Elizabeth, the man you saw visiting her regularly was definitely an *Englischer?"* Ettie asked. "Or could you be mistaken about that?"

"Jah. No mistake. He was wearing a suit and driving a car. I didn't know him. My neighbor on the other side of Paula told me he let the police know about Paula's visitor. I didn't talk with the police at all."

"Would you recognize him if you saw him somewhere else, or if we had a photograph of him?"

She shook her head. "My distance sight is not very good, but my close-up vision is. I'm not sure if that's called longsighted or shortsighted. I think it's shortsighted."

"I'm the opposite. I need my reading glasses these days to do my knitting," Elsa-May said. "I haven't done much lately."

Ettie noticed Elsa-May glance down at her fingers, at the knuckles that were growing larger. She hadn't mentioned anything to her, but Ettie was certain that Elsa-May's fingers were giving her pain. That was likely the real reason she hadn't knitted much lately.

"I'm sorry I wasn't very nice to either of you yesterday. I was just so upset about Paula—that someone could do this to her. I'll help you in whatever way I can."

"You've been such a good help already," Ettie said.

Elsa-May leaned forward. "Did you ever happen to see a woman visit Paula—an *Englischer?*"

"Nee never."

"And you're home most of the time, aren't you?"

"I don't go out that much—not too often these days."

"Right. That's good to know."

Elizabeth looked at the cake. "Would you take the rest of the cake with you? I can't eat it all by myself. It's nice to have a slice every now and again, but I wouldn't eat any more of it."

"Keep it here for visitors," Ettie said.

"I don't get many people dropping by. You'd get more visitors than I would because there's the two of you."

"Okay, *denke,* we'll take it, but only if you're sure," Elsa-May added, "and if you'll keep a slice for yourself to have tomorrow."

"Okay. Aren't the police closer to finding out who attacked Paula? It's been over a day already."

"I hope so. They won't know much more until all the evidence comes in. I believe there are fingerprints they found on what was used to hit Paula."

Elsa-May added, "And, of course, the plate number you wrote down would be of interest to them."

"*Jah.* I'll get that for you now." Elizabeth went into the other room and moments later returned with a slip of paper.

Ettie and Elsa-May left Elizabeth's house with stomachs full of tea and cake, and with the plate number held tightly in Ettie's hand. Elsa-May carried the box with the rest of the cake.

"I think we should go to see Detective Kelly now."

"*Jah,* he would like to know who the car belongs to."

Ettie shook her head. "I just don't see that Paula's visitor would've attacked her. He would know the neighbors would have seen him coming and going."

"I don't see what you're saying. They might have argued about something and he hit her without giving it too much thought—in anger."

"*Nee,* Elsa-May, that makes no sense. They were arguing and then in a rage he went to his car and got the tire iron? And then went back and hit her? *Nee!* That's silly."

Elsa-May nodded. "*Jah,* I agree, that doesn't make sense. I can see now that it must've been planned."

Ettie nodded. "It had to be premeditated and done in a fit of rage. That would be my guess."

"That seems so."

"Elsa-May?"

"Jah?"

"What's a tire iron?"

Elsa-May pushed out her lips and thought for a while. "I have no idea."

"Is it the thing that holds the car up while the tires are being changed?"

"I think that's called a jack."

"Is it the thing that tire bolts are loosened and tightened with?"

"I'm not certain. It sounds likely. It could be what you said. I can't think what else it could be."

"When the taxi gets here we'll ask the driver so we'll be sure what it is before we see Kelly. If we ask Detective Kelly what it is, he'll have some sarcastic comment to make about us not knowing."

"Good idea. Kelly spoke as if we'd know what one was. We can't disappoint him."

Ettie nodded.

Chapter 5

Later that same day, Ettie and Elsa-May were told there would be a long wait to see Detective Kelly. While they sat in the large waiting area, a lady joined them, sitting close by.

After a moment, the woman spoke to them. "Excuse me, but are you friends of a woman called Paula Peters?"

"Yes, we are," Ettie said. "Do you know her?"

"No, I don't know her at all, but they've brought me in to question me about her."

Elsa-May and Ettie looked at each other.

The woman continued, "They found my locket in her house. I told the police I reported it stolen weeks ago and even put in an insurance claim for it." A tear rolled down her face.

Ettie leaned over and introduced herself and her sister.

"Nice to meet you. My name's Nora George." She sniffed and pulled a tissue out of her pocket.

"I've never had any dealings with the police before."

Elsa-May said, "I'm sure it's just a misunderstanding that will be sorted out soon."

"No it won't. They didn't believe me about the locket."

"You said you reported it stolen so there'll be a record of it."

"There would. If they look for it, they'll find it. I can't remember the exact date I reported it stolen."

"Just tell them what you told us and everything will be fine," Elsa-May said.

Nora wiped her nose. "They looked in my car and found my tire iron missing and they said it would be the same kind of tire iron that they found at Paula Peters' house."

"I'm sure there would be thousands of them out there and when they find that your prints aren't on it they'll know you didn't do it," Ettie said.

"I didn't even know I had a tire iron. They tell me there's one in every car. My husband looks after all those things. He's at work now." She looked down at her wringing hands as though they belonged to someone else. "I hope I don't have to tell him about this."

"Just tell them what you told us and I'm sure everything will be fine."

"This way please, Mrs. George."

Ettie and Elsa-May looked up to see two uniformed police officers. Nora stood and they escorted her down the corridor where the interview rooms were.

"So it was her locket?" Elsa-May said.

"Jah."

"Someone stole it she said."

"The poor woman. She looks terrified. I don't know if she was more scared of the police or her husband finding out she's being questioned by the police."

It was an hour later that Detective Kelly walked the elderly sisters into his office.

When they sat opposite him, Ettie said, "How's Paula?"

59

"There's been no change I'm afraid. Now, do you have anything for me?"

"We've lots of information for you," Ettie said.

He smiled. "Excellent!"

"We found out from Elizabeth next door…"

Elsa-May leaned forward. "You were right, Detective, she talked to us more today."

"Please, Elsa-May, I was speaking and you just talked right over the top of me."

"Sorry." Elsa-May frowned at Ettie. "Well, go on—he's listening."

"Now, where was I?"

The detective said, "You were telling me you've got some information." He raised his eyebrows.

"Elizabeth, Paula's neighor, told us that Paula had a frequent visitor who was always wearing a suit."

"You gave me that yesterday. Do you have anything new? Please say you have something else to tell me? Before you answer that, would your friend be able to identify this man in a lineup?"

"No," Ettie answered.

Elsa-May added, "She can't see too well over long distances."

He pushed himself back in his chair. "That's no help at all. She'd be ripped apart in a trial."

"What trial? I don't think Elizabeth would ever go into a courtroom."

"Forget I said anything. I was more or less giving voice to my scattered thoughts." He made a circling motion with his hand near his head.

Ettie continued, "We know something else."

"Go on."

"We were driving to Elizabeth's place in a taxi and the driver told us that he drove a woman there recently, and she asked to be dropped at the end of the street."

"Did you get the driver's phone number?"

Ettie pulled the cake receipt, with the driver's name and ID written on it, from her sleeve and placed it on the desk.

"Hello," the detective said as he reached for it. "Good work, you two. What else do you have up your sleeve, a cup of coffee? I could do with one right now."

"No!"

"Anything else?" he asked.

Elsa-May said, "We met a woman in the waiting area; her name's Nora George."

"She's the owner of the locket," Ettie said.

Kelly grimaced. "I know that, but how did you find that out?"

"She told us."

"She's a talker then, that's good. She might tell us what we need to know."

Ettie said, "You don't think she harmed Paula, do you?"

"My team identified the photo in the locket by scanning the image through some new fangled facial-imaging software, and two possible matches came up. One man was dead, and we tracked the other through his furniture store website where he has an image of himself on the home page."

"So the man in the locket photo knows you brought his wife in?" Elsa-May asked.

"Yes. He was the one who told us where she was."

Ettie said, "That's funny. The woman didn't know her husband knew about it."

"We find it best not to give them too much information when we bring them in for questioning—it keeps them nervous."

"That's not nice, Detective."

"Ettie, my job has nothing to do with being nice. I'm not a social director. My job is to keep society safe and lock the bad guys up—remember?"

"Nora said she didn't do it. She even reported that locket stolen."

He shook his head. "That's what she told us. We checked into her story and there's no record of her ever reporting it, or anything else, stolen—either to the police or her insurance company."

"She's such a tiny woman and Paula wasn't small. It seems unlikely that Nora would be able to overpower a much bigger woman."

"Are you forgetting the tire iron, Mrs. Smith?"

Ettie stared at the detective.

"Now if you ladies will leave the job to the professionals, I've got some business to attend to."

"What are you going to do about that?" Ettie tapped on the taxi driver's ID and name.

He frowned, picked up the paper and stared at it closely. "There are too many digits." He looked up at Ettie. "Don't tell me you got this from the woman with the bad eyesight?"

Ettie's shoulders drooped as she nodded.

"Okay, leave it with me. We'll run a check and see what we can come up with." When he picked up the phone to speak with someone, Ettie and Elsa-May took that as their cue to leave.

The sisters made their way through the police station and out the front door of the building. When they were halfway down the front steps of the station, Kelly caught up with them.

"Ladies, we've struck gold!"

"What is it?" Ettie nearly overbalanced as she made an attempt to swing around to look at him. Detective Kelly grabbed her arm to steady her. "Thank you, Detective. What is it you've found out?"

"That woman you met in the waiting area—Nora

64

George..."

"Yes we know that," Elsa-May said.

"That's what she said her name was."

The detective drew in a sharp breath. "Nora's husband's plate number is remarkably similar to the number you just gave me. All we had to do is lose the last number and turn one of the zeros into an eight."

"So it was Nora's husband who was visiting Paula?" Elsa-May asked.

He nodded. "Right, and what's more, I've just been informed we got an anonymous tip off our hotline. Nora George was overheard telling someone her husband was having an affair, and Nora claimed she was going to find his mistress and kill her."

Ettie and Elsa-May gasped.

"This has certainly made my job a lot easier," the detective said.

"Oh dear," Ettie said.

Elsa-May looked at Ettie and said, "It seems like that poor Nora woman is in trouble."

Kelly looked pleased. "I'll bring her husband in and see what he has to say."

Ettie shook her head. "Nora won't like that."

"No; she didn't want her husband to know."

Kelly scoffed. "Too bad. Anyway, I'm glad I caught you before you left. I thought you'd like an update."

"Yes, we did."

"We appreciate it," Elsa-May said.

"Well, keep asking around and see what else you find out. It's not over until it's over." Kelly turned back and sprinted up the top two steps, then disappeared into the station.

Ettie and Elsa-May hung onto the railing staring at each other.

"Well, that's an interesting turn of events, Ettie."

"*Jah,* and the woman didn't know her husband knew about it when he was the one who told them where she was. I don't like the sound of that. He doesn't sound nice at all."

"You think he would've dropped everything and come here to be with her."

"Exactly. She was dreadfully worried and her husband should've known she'd be upset."

"Let's go home and rest. We've had a long and tiring day."

Chapter 6

The next day the sisters went back to see Detective Kelly, who had more news for them.

"The fingerprints on the tire iron belong to Nora George." He closed his office door and sat behind his desk.

Ettie said, "Nora said her husband looked after the car and the maintenance of it. It sounded to me like she would've never touched the tire iron."

"I'll go and set her free, shall I?" the detective said with more than a hint of sarcasm.

"Maybe she had occasion to touch the tool—the tire iron—and that's why her prints were on it. It doesn't mean she's guilty," Elsa-May said.

Ettie continued, "If she'd been the one to do the attack, why would she have left it behind? Everyone knows about fingerprints and DNA and the like."

"Would you allow us to speak with Nora?" Elsa-May asked.

Kelly laughed. "What do you expect her to say? She'll say she's innocent. Everyone's innocent; didn't you know that?"

"We believe her," Ettie said.

"Oh, then it must be true!" He shook his head at them.

"Can we speak with her?" Elsa-May repeated.

"No! Definitely not! We've interviewed her enough, and besides, we need everything on tape."

"What harm would it do if we talk with her?" Elsa-May asked.

"Unless you're her lawyer there's no point. Have you gotten your law degree since we last spoke?"

"Of course not," Elsa-May scoffed. "Is she allowed visitors?"

"No! She's being transferred from here in a couple of days and she'll remain in prison until her court case."

"What about bail?" Ettie asked.

"Her bail was set at two hundred thousand dollars."

"That's a lot of money! What about her husband?

Didn't he bail her out?"

"She's still here. It's a lot of money and he'd have to come up with ten percent of the full amount for the bail bondsman. That would be twenty thousand and not many people have immediate access to that kind of money."

"Have you interviewed the husband yet?"

"Yes. We did interview Cameron George yesterday. He's previously been in law enforcement. He's quite a nice fellow, and he had no idea his wife was capable of such a thing. The poor man's devastated by the whole thing. He admitted to us that he had an affair with Paula Peters some time ago—that's not against the law. It's morally wrong but not criminally."

"It goes to show what kind of person he is," Elsa-May said.

"By whose standards?" Kelly asked.

"Society's standards." Elsa-May looked Kelly directly in the eyes.

He looked away. "Seems Nora found out her husband had an affair with Paula, and maybe thought it was ongoing. She tried to do away with her competition. It's a crime of passion."

"Wouldn't you let us speak with her?" Ettie asked.

Elsa-May added, "What harm could it possibly do if we spoke with her? We've agreed to help you all we can with information, so it would only help us if we heard directly from her and listened to what she has to say."

The detective's face turned beet red. "For the last time, no! And nothing you can do or say will make me change my mind."

Ten minutes later, Kelly led Ettie and Elsa-May into the lock-up area of the station. He snarled at them, "This is against our policy, so you'll have to make it quick."

He nodded to the cells. "She's in the end one."

Ettie and Elsa-May walked past two empty cells before they reached the one where Nora George was being held.

Nora was sitting slumped on a bench, and she sprang to her feet when she saw them. "You've come to visit me?"

"We have."

"Do you know where my husband is?"

"Hasn't he been to see you?"

"I don't need him to *see* me, I need him to bail me out."

"He might be trying to raise the money. They said he'd need ten percent of the bail money."

"He can borrow it against the house. I spoke with him not long after I arrived here and asked him to get me out. I haven't heard from him since." Tears rolled down her face.

"Don't be upset. I'm sure there's just some mistake and it'll be sorted out soon."

"They think I did it. They think I killed a woman that I don't even know."

"Did your husband know her?"

"No! Not that I'm aware of. If he knew her, he would've said so. Can you please go and see my husband and tell him to get me out of here? They won't let me make any more calls. Tell him to borrow the money. I don't know why he hasn't gotten me out already."

"Okay," Ettie agreed. It was clear that Detective Kelly hadn't told Nora all he knew about her husband.

Nora continued, "I can't believe this can happen to an innocent person. I was minding my own business and the police arrested me."

"We'll help you all we can," Ettie said

Nora gave Ettie and Elsa-May her address.

"Will you remember that, Ettie?" Elsa-May asked.

"You remember the street name and I'll remember the street number."

Chapter 7

Ettie stood close while Elsa-May knocked on the door of Mr. George's house.

A woman came to the door. She stood staring at the two of them and no one said a word for a good five seconds. The woman had a pretty face. Her hair was black and cut bluntly at her chin; her skin was creamy and her eyes were nearly as dark as her hair.

"Yes?" the woman finally said.

Ettie cleared her throat. "We're here to see Mr. George. Is he at home?"

"Who wants to see him?" The woman wedged herself in the doorway so they couldn't see inside.

"We know Mrs. George, and she sent us here to give him a message."

"Wait a minute," she said before she closed the door.

Ettie and Elsa-May looked at each other.

"Is she getting him?" Ettie asked.

"I think so. She told us to wait and she wouldn't have done that if she wanted us to go away."

A few moments later, the door opened again and a dark-haired tall man stood in the doorway. "Hello?"

"Are you Mr. George?"

"Yes. What's this about?"

"We've just come from speaking with your wife. She's very distressed and she asked us to give you a message."

He dipped his head. "What is it?"

"She's very distressed, as I said, and she wants you to bail her out. She said you could borrow against the house."

"It's not as easy as that," he said. "There are other circumstances."

"Like what?" Ettie asked.

"I'm afraid I can't say, but if you're talking to my wife again, tell her that I've got a good lawyer for her. He's a friend of mine, and he owes me a favor."

Ettie pulled her mouth to one side. "I don't think

we'll be speaking with her again."

He looked at Ettie and then at Elsa-May. "I'm sorry—who are you people?"

"We're friends of the woman who was injured and we happened to bump into your wife at the police station and she told us what happened," Ettie said.

"And she also told us how the police think she did it because of the locket that was found in our friend's house," Elsa-May said.

Ettie nodded. "Yes. The locket that she'd reported stolen."

He shook his head. "You shouldn't get yourselves involved. My wife is a storyteller. That locket was never stolen like she told the police. I even checked with the insurance company and no claim was ever made. I'll do the best I can for her, but I can't do the impossible."

"Do you know Paula Peters?" Ettie asked, to see if he'd be open and honest.

"Yes, of course. I employed her in my furniture store up until just over a year ago."

"Can I ask who the lady is who answered the door?" Elsa-May asked.

Mr. George laughed. "You two do have a lot of questions. That's my business partner, Casey Campbell. We're going over a few details to finalize our next promotion, if that was the next thing you were going to ask."

"We only came to give you the message from your wife since she's no longer allowed to call anyone."

He shook his head. "I'm doing all I can. If you'll excuse me, I've got work to do."

"We won't hold you up," Elsa-May said abruptly.

When the man closed the door, Ettie and Elsa-May walked back to the sidewalk in front of his house.

"Do you think the police know that Nora's husband had employed Paula?"

"*Jah!* Well, come to think of it, the man admitted about the affair, but Kelly didn't let us know that Cameron George was her employer at the time. Maybe Kelly doesn't know, but don't forget he doesn't tell us everything. They think Nora attacked Paula because she suspected her husband was having an affair with her. That seems clear from what we've learned so far. I can't work out why the detective doesn't tell us everything."

"He never does," Elsa-May said. "But if he wants our help with people in the community he should let us in on everything."

"That's just the way he is and he's not likely to change. If Nora didn't attack Paula, then who did?"

"Who would've had reason to want her dead?"

"Surely if Paula had been having an affair with Nora's husband, she would've stopped after she joined the community," Ettie said.

"One would hope so!"

"What will we do now?"

"Let's go and visit the Lapps again and hopefully they'll be home this time."

The ladies headed for the nearest public phone to call for a taxi.

* * *

That afternoon, Ettie and Elsa-May were sitting across the kitchen table from Mr. and Mrs. Lapp

"They tell us they have the person who did this to Paula and she's a woman," Mrs. Lapp said.

"They could be wrong, though," Elsa-May said.

"We just have to hope Paula recovers so she can say who attacked her, in case they have the wrong person," Ettie said.

Boris Lapp peered at Ettie. "Do you think they have arrested the wrong person?"

"I do. There are too many things that just don't add up."

"Is that a car?" Elsa-May said.

"I think so." Mrs. Lapp stood up and looked out the window. "It looks like it might be a policeman, but he's not wearing a uniform."

Elsa-May and Ettie looked at each other and knew it had to be Detective Kelly. He'd asked for their help so he couldn't be mad at them for speaking with the Lapp family, could he?

Elsa-May stood beside Diane Lapp and looked out the window. "That is a police detective. It's

Detective Kelly," Elsa-May said.

Boris and Diane went to their front door and waited for the detective with Ettie and Elsa-May not far behind.

"I'm not going to talk with him," Boris Lapp said.

"He's all right," Ettie said. "It'll be better if you speak with him."

"Hello," Kelly said when he looked up and saw them at the door.

"Afternoon, Detective," Boris said. "Can we help you with something? We've already told the police all we know, which is nothing."

"I hope for your sake that's true, but it's your son I'd like to speak with. I'd like him to come down to the station to answer some questions."

"Which one? We've got eight sons," Diane answered.

"The son who claims to be Paula Peters' boyfriend."

Boris and Diane Lapp looked at each other.

"That'll be Obadiah, our youngest," Boris said,

"but he's not able to answer questions by himself."

"Is he over eighteen?"

"Yes, he is."

"Then he's capable of answering questions."

"What Mr. Lapp means is that Obadiah is not like a regular person of his age. He's more like someone younger. His mind is that of a ten to twelve-year-old," Ettie said before she looked at Diane who had turned around to look at her. "Is that right?" she asked the Lapps.

"What Ettie says is right. He's a simple boy and he's not got much idea of what's going on," Diane said.

"Relax! I'm not going to arrest him or anything. I just need to ask him a couple of questions. There's a woman under arrest already for the assault on Paula Peters."

"Ettie and Elsa-May were just telling us that they think you've got the wrong person, so how do we know you're not going to accuse our boy of doing it? He wouldn't know how to answer your questions. He might even admit to doing something if it's put into his mind. He doesn't know reality from stories sometimes."

Kelly glared at Ettie and Elsa-May. "What these two ladies have told you is merely their opinion and isn't based on fact. We have the perpetrator in custody—that part is correct. We're just after more information."

The detective smiled then, and Ettie was relieved that he wasn't mad with them for interfering.

The detective turned his attention to Boris Lapp. "You're welcome to come and sit with him while he's being questioned."

"No! You're not taking him anywhere and he's not going to be questioned." Boris folded his arms in front of him while he stared at Detective Kelly's startled face.

"Perhaps you don't want me to talk with your son because he's got something to hide."

"I'm not saying any more." Boris tried to close the door, but, as quick as a flash, Detective Kelly put a shiny leather-shod toe in the way.

"Where was your son in the early hours of the

twelfth?" Kelly barked out.

"Here at home with us," Diane replied.

"Can you be certain?" Kelly asked.

Boris opened the door wider and took a step forward, forcing Kelly to step back. He towered over Kelly by a good four inches. "He was here at home with us," he repeated. "Is he under arrest?"

"No." Detective Kelly said.

Boris backed inside and closed the door on the detective. He turned around, and said to Ettie and Elsa-May, "If they're not going to arrest him, they can't make him talk."

A moment later, Ettie was relieved when she heard the detective's car head down the drive.

"They might not leave things there," Elsa-May said. "You might have made him more determined to talk with Obadiah."

Boris walked to the window and looked out. "I hope that's the last we see of him."

"I wonder how he heard that Obadiah thought Paula was his girlfriend," Diane said.

"I'm afraid that I mentioned that to him. I'm so

sorry, but I didn't think he'd come here like this and ask to see Obadiah. I told him what Obadiah was like," Ettie said.

"Don't blame yourself, Ettie, you weren't to know what the policeman would do," Boris said.

Elsa-May added, "He's a detective. Anyway, he's arrested someone so I don't think he considers Obadiah's guilty of anything. I'm certain he just wanted to question Obadiah about Paula. Maybe Obadiah knows something about Paula if the two of them were close."

Boris chuckled. "They weren't close except in Obadiah's head. Paula barely spoke to Obadiah the whole time she was here, and he was so scared of her that he didn't say much to her."

"Nee, the police wouldn't find anything out by talking with Obadiah," Diane said.

"Where is Obadiah today?" Elsa-May asked.

"He's probably in the barn. That's where he stays mostly, if he's not with the rest of the boys."

When Ettie and Elsa-May left the Lapps' home, Ettie knew they would have to speak with Kelly alone and find out why he'd come to speak with Obadiah. Had the detective realized that he'd made a mistake by arresting Nora George, and was he looking further afield?

Chapter 8

After Elsa-May and Ettie had rested from their visit with the Lapps, Ettie was still disturbed about Detective Kelly showing so much interest in Obadiah.

"We must go back and see Detective Kelly."

"We talked about it earlier and that's what we decided to do." Elsa-May gave a sharp nod.

"Last time we were at the police station, he had Nora locked up so why was he trying to ask Obadiah questions?"

"Maybe it's because you opened your big mouth and made mentioned of Obadiah."

Ettie's jaw fell open in shock.

Elsa-May continued, "You were the one who told detective Kelly you didn't think Nora George was guilty. So that's put a doubt in his mind to start with, and then he's clearly realized things don't add up."

"Surely he can't be still holding Nora in jail then."

"They're not going to release her just like that. They'd need some kind of proof that either she was innocent or another person was guilty."

"It was odd to visit Nora's husband. He didn't seem too concerned that his wife was in prison. He was working with his business partner just like it was any other day. And as you said, Kelly must've known that Paula had worked for him before she joined our community."

"I must say I find it quite annoying that he wants your help, Ettie, and then he doesn't tell you everything."

Ettie pressed her lips firmly together. "I know what you mean. It would be much easier if he told us things up front. He only tells us what he wants us to know."

"It seems to me that if Nora had suspected her husband was having an affair with Paula, why wouldn't she suspect the business partner of having an affair with him also? Yet didn't Nora tell us that she didn't know Paula?"

"Yes, she did," Ettie said. "Perhaps she was telling the truth and she really didn't know Paula. She might not know all the people her husband employs."

"Mr. George and his business partner sure looked cozy together. And the business partner was quite attractive."

"Then that's what we'll have to tell the detective," Ettie said.

"What will we tell him? We don't know anything. It didn't turn out too well opening your big mouth about Obadiah, did it?"

Ettie pouted. "Well that's how these things work. The detective goes down one avenue with the investigation until he's exhausted it, and then he goes down another one."

"I suppose you're right. So are we visiting Kelly again today or not?"

"Yes we will."

Before they left for the police station, Ettie and Elsa-May called the hospital and found out that there was no change in Paula's condition.

Just as they were getting out of the taxi at the police station, they saw that Kelly was pulling out of the parking lot. They flagged him down.

"When will you be back?" Ettie asked him after he rolled down his window.

"I haven't got time to talk now, there have been some new developments. I'll fill you in on them later today. I'll come to your house."

The detective zoomed away in his car and Elsa-May and Ettie stared after him.

"What do you think that was about?" Elsa-May asked.

"I've got no idea."

"Do you think we need some new furniture, Elsa-May?"

"You know how I feel about furniture. The furniture we have is from our parents and their parents before them, except for your new couch. I thought you agreed that suits us just fine."

"I said 'furniture,' Elsa-May, and that means we have to go to a 'furniture store,' and just maybe we might find ourselves at the furniture store of a certain Mr. George."

"Ah, I see. *Jah,* it wouldn't hurt to look for some new furniture."

"Exactly and that doesn't mean we have to buy any." Ettie chuckled.

"Where is his furniture store?"

"Why don't we go back into the station and ask to borrow their phone book?" Ettie suggested.

"Good idea."

They borrowed the phone book and looked up all the furniture stores in the area.

"This sounds likely—George's Furniture. It has to be that one," Ettie said.

"It's highly likely."

"I hope so."

Elsa-May borrowed pen and paper and scribbled down the address. The furniture store was only a ten minute drive away.

They got out of the taxi and walked inside the huge barn of a place.

After looking from one end of the store to the other, they couldn't see Mr. George or his business partner anywhere.

"I wonder if we've got the correct store," Elsa-May whispered to Ettie.

When a young woman approached them and asked if they needed any help, Ettie responded by saying, "Would Mr. George happen to be working in the store today?"

"Or Ms. Campbell?" Elsa-May interjected.

"Mr. George and Ms. Campbell have gone to a furniture expo."

"That's a shame we've missed them. When will they be back?" Elsa-May asked.

"I have no idea. I'm sorry. Can I help you with anything?"

"No thank you. When did they leave? We were only talking to him a day or two ago and he didn't mention that he wasn't going to be here today," Elsa-May said.

"He left this morning. Shall I tell him you stopped by to see him?"

Elsa-May shook her head. "No, I wouldn't trouble you to go to that bother."

Ettie added, "We'll call in and see him another day."

"Where did you say he went?" Elsa-May asked.

"Boston." The young woman smiled at them.

"Thank you." Ettie and Elsa-May hurried out of the store.

"What do you think of that, Ettie? That's probably why Kelly was in such a hurry."

"Yes. Kelly has figured out that Mr. George wanted his wife out of the way so he could be with his business partner. Cameron George framed his wife for murder. It was fortunate for Paula that he thought she was dead."

"Well, that's not quite what I was thinking, but it does make sense. It would clear the way for him to be with his business partner, but why would he want Paula out of the way? The affair was finished with a long time ago."

"I don't know," Elsa-May said.

"Why would he leave town if he's innocent?"

Ettie asked.

"*Jah.* That sure makes him look guilty."

"I don't think he's gone permanently. He wouldn't just up and leave his store like that. He wouldn't do that."

"So you think he's coming back and not running away?" Elsa-May asked.

Ettie nodded.

"Unless, of course, he already told the detective that he was going away for a few days."

"*Jah*, that would make him appear innocent while his wife continues to suffer in jail." Ettie sighed. "We won't know anything now until Detective Kelly lets us know. I wish he wouldn't ask us to help him with his cases and then keep us out of things. It's very difficult."

"Come on, Ettie, we've done all we can. Let's go home."

"Kelly did say he'd stop by the house later today. I hope he remembers."

Ettie went home in the taxi with her sister, wishing there was more she could do. It upset her greatly that Nora George was sitting in prison for a crime she didn't do while Mr. George was off on a business trip with his business partner.

Chapter 9

Just before dinnertime, Detective Kelly knocked on the door of Ettie and Elsa-May's house.

"Come in, Detective," Elsa-May said when she opened the door and saw him standing there.

He looked around and especially about Elsa-May's feet. "Have you got that attack dog of yours locked up? This is a new suit."

Elsa-May chuckled. "I've closed Snowy outside, so it's quite safe."

The corners of the detective's lips twitched as he walked into the house.

Ettie came hurrying out of the kitchen to greet him. "Do you have news of Paula?"

"I've just come from the hospital. The outcome might not be good even if she comes out of the coma. The specialist I spoke with said she's got youth on her side. Then he rattled off a string of statistics, and then to sum things up he said she might suffer nerve damage, memory loss, or seizures. The worst-case scenario, of course, is that she might never wake up at all."

Ettie said, "Shouldn't you allow her family in to see her in that case?"

"We'll see." He scratched the side of his face.

"You'd have to—surely," Elsa-May said.

"I didn't come here to be lectured. I came here to tell you something."

"Come and sit down," Ettie said. "We've been waiting for you to tell us what happened today."

Kelly sat down with them and Elsa-May said, "We went to George's furniture store today."

He frowned, looking none too happy. "You did?"

The sisters nodded.

"And what did you find out?"

"We found out that Mr. George and his business partner have gone to Boston."

"Yes, I know that. We have a tail on him."

"You do?"

He smiled. "Yes, I do."

"So, you're suspicious of him?" Ettie asked.

"It doesn't hurt to keep eyes and ears open. I

didn't ask him not to leave town and he was under no obligation to inform me that he was going anywhere. He's got a return ticket for two days time."

"Meanwhile his wife's rotting in a prison cell," Elsa-May said in disgust.

"Yes, while he's away on a business trip with an attractive woman," Ettie added

"Mr. George said he got his wife a good lawyer. I suppose he's trying to look like he's doing something," Ettie said.

"You spoke with him?" Kelly asked.

Ettie and Elsa-May looked at each other and Ettie said, "We went to his house because he wasn't coming to see his wife."

"Nora asked us to," Elsa-May said.

"If she asked you to jump off a cliff, would you?" He shook his head.

"We went to his house and the business partner was there," Elsa-May said.

Changing the subject to calm Kelly down, Ettie asked, "What's the lawyer like that Cameron

George got for his wife. Is he a good lawyer?"

Detective Kelly shook his head. "The man's a drunk, and he's nearly been disbarred twice."

"That's dreadful!" Elsa-May said.

Kelly nodded.

"So, he's not a good lawyer?" Ettie asked. "Or did he do things to help his clients?"

"He's not a good lawyer at all. I don't know how he'll get past the fact that her prints were the only ones on the tire iron and the locket."

After a moment of silence, Elsa-May said, "Ettie has a theory. Go on, tell him, Ettie."

"Okay. What if Nora's husband had intended to kill Paula and frame his wife for her murder? That way, his wife would be out of the way so he would be free to carry on with his business partner?"

The detective coughed and then smiled at the two of them. "Usually people divorce."

"Yes, but if his wife went to jail that would restrict her from getting a decent settlement—would it not?"

"How do you know about things like that, Ettie?"

Kelly asked.

"I overhear things. Am I right?"

"I think you are. It'd be easier for him to get a divorce and she wouldn't be in a position to do much about it, but why would he want Paula out of the way?"

Elsa-May added, "She might have had some information about him, or possibly his store."

Ettie took over, "And that way, he would've been getting rid of two birds with one stone. And…"

Elsa-May interrupted, "What if he were the one who rang in that anonymous tip that they overhead Nora wanted to kill the person her husband was having an affair with."

"It's possible," the detective said. "It was a woman who called in, but he could've put someone up to it."

"Yes, he could've paid someone to call," Elsa-May said.

"The mistake he made was that Paula wasn't dead."

"And thank goodness for that." Detective Kelly

sighed. "You think that Nora's husband attacked Paula with the tire iron that only had his wife's prints on it, and then he dropped the locket at the scene of the crime? He also must've had the foresight to steal the locket from his wife weeks before?"

"Yes, he would've planned it all." Ettie nodded. "That's right."

"It sounds like it was his car in the street, but no one ever saw Nora in the street."

"What you're forgetting is that Nora lied to us. There was no claim lodged with the insurance company and no police report was made—ever. I'll be speaking with your taxi driver first thing in the morning and I'll see what he has to say about the woman he delivered to Paula's street."

"That's good. I've been meaning to ask you about that."

Kelly asked. "What makes you think he was having an affair, or is having an affair, with his business partner?"

Elsa-May said, "According to Nora, her husband

102

was having an affair with someone."

"Did she admit that to you?"

"No, but you said that she told someone that."

"Elsa-May, haven't you been listening? The detective just agreed that Cameron George might have put someone up to making that phone call about his wife—the tip that came into the hotline."

Kelly nodded. "We can't place much store on hearsay, it would be helpful if we could find someone to testify that Nora suspected her husband of having an affair."

"Who?" Elsa-May asked.

"I don't know yet. Cameron George himself admitted the affair with Paula, but what makes you think he's having an affair with his business partner?" Kelly asked.

"They looked like there was something between them," Elsa-May said.

"We need more than that," Kelly answered. "We need proof. And even if he's having an affair with someone, it doesn't mean that he framed his wife for murder."

Ettie and Elsa-May glanced at one another.

Kelly said, "Theories are well and good, and I'm happy to listen to them, but there's no escaping the fact that we've got solid evidence that it was Nora George who attacked Paula."

"Nora looks too sweet and too small to cause anyone harm."

Ettie frowned at Elsa-May's reasoning.

"It's all too obvious. The fingerprints on the weapon that was all too conveniently left in clear view; then there was the locket, which obviously would've been traced back to Nora," Ettie said.

The detective nodded. "Yes, my job's usually not that easy. I'll investigate other avenues to satisfy the lingering doubt I have." He shook his head. "It sure would've helped if Nora had an alibi for the time Paula was attacked."

"She was alone?" Elsa-May asked.

"Where was her husband?"

"He was on a business trip and he was able to show us a receipt from the hotel."

"Was he alone in that hotel?"

"He said his business partner was with him. He was quick to point out they had separate rooms."

"Was he close enough so he could've driven through the night and back again?" Ettie asked.

"Yes, as a matter of fact, he was. Just to satisfy you, I'll run a check on car-rental companies. He wouldn't have used his own car, I wouldn't think, if that had been the case."

"Thank you."

"Detective Kelly, I've been wondering something. What did Nora say when you told her there was no report of the locket being stolen?" Elsa-May asked.

Kelly's face soured. "She admitted to lying— said she was nervous, but she maintains the locket had been missing for some time."

"Nora might be telling the truth," Ettie said.

"If that's so, she shouldn't have lied. She's got no evidence to back up her claims and she lied during questioning. That's not good." He shook his head.

"Would you like to stay for dinner, Detective? We've made far too much for just us two."

"I'd love to. I smelled it when I first came in."

Over dinner, Kelly said, "Do you know what we found when we searched the Georges' house?"

"No. You never told us that you searched their house at all."

"It's standard procedure. The woman's going on trial for murder and we need as much evidence as we can get to back it up."

"What did you find?" Ettie asked, wondering whether the house was searched before or after they had visited the Georges' residence and found him there with the business partner.

"We took three laptops out of the house and on those laptops we found various emails between Cameron George and many different women he'd been having affairs with over the years. We didn't ask him, but it was apparent from the emails. Paula Peters was one of those women while she was working at the furniture store. She ended things shortly after the current business partner appeared on the scene."

"That lined up with what you knew."

"Yes. We also found various sites and Internet searches on how to implicate someone in a murder."

"You mean, frame them for a murder?"

"Exactly. And that was on Mr. George's computer, which was password protected. But, of course, my team technicians were able to get past that small obstacle."

"That's why you're listening to our theory? That's why you're starting to believe us that Nora's husband might have something to do with this after all?"

He nodded. "That's something we're now looking into."

Elsa-May set her knife and fork down against her plate. "Didn't you say Cameron George used to be a police officer?"

Kelly nodded.

"Then he would've known exactly what he was doing. He would know the very things that would make his wife appear guilty."

He nodded again.

Elsa-May asked, "Have you spoken to his

business partner? She might have some information to give you."

"Yes, we did. She denied having an affair with Cameron George until we told her that we'd found the emails that had gone back and forth between the two of them. When she knew we had those, she admitted it."

"Detective Kelly!"

"We just talked about that moments ago and you made us appear silly for thinking she was having an affair with Cameron." Elsa-May glared at the detective.

"You're right." He loaded his fork with chicken.

"Is that all you have to say to us?" Ettie asked.

Kelly lowered his fork. "Okay, you got me. I just want you to know only what you need to know. It would be helpful if you would tell me what I need to know. I ask you questions and you find the answers for me—and nothing more."

Ettie exhaled. "Sometimes that's not so easy."

"Particularly when you've got someone in jail for a crime they didn't commit," Elsa-May added.

Kelly popped the chicken into his mouth while the two sisters stared at him. When he finished chewing he said, "All right, point taken. Casey Campbell told us that Cameron told her he was leaving his wife."

"That's exactly what he told Paula."

"Yes, and every other woman he had been involved with and we've got the emails to prove it. Anyway, Casey said the thing that was holding him up was that he knew he'd lose a lot of the money in the divorce." Kelly looked down at his food.

"What's wrong detective?" Elsa-May asked.

"Why do women believe men like him when they never intend to leave their wives at all?" he asked.

Ettie shook her head. "I don't know, but in Cameron George's case, it seems he found a way of getting his wife out of the way and keeping all or most of his money."

Elsa-May added, "Yes, in one way, or another. His wife being in jail was a way to get her out of the picture."

Kelly waved a hand in the air. "Spare me the details. I know what you think; you've told me often enough."

Ettie leaned forward and set her gaze on the detective. "So when are you going to believe us? You've got enough evidence."

"No, I haven't!"

Just when they'd finished dinner, they had another guest arrive. It was the retired detective, Ronald Crowley.

"Come in and sit down. We've got Detective Kelly here," Ettie said.

"Yes, I saw his car outside." Crowley took one step inside and looked into the living room of the small house.

The detectives nodded to one another, and then Kelly got up to shake hands.

"I've heard what happened to the Amish woman," Crowley said once everyone had sat down.

"Is that why you're here?" Kelly asked.

"Yes."

Kelly crossed one leg over the other. "Do you

want a story?"

"I'd love one. There's nothing like trying to solve a good mystery and from the expression on your faces you're all baffled about something."

Elsa-May leaned forward, "Not baffled, disturbed."

Ettie asked, "Before the story begins, would you like some dessert, Ronald?"

"Have you had dinner?" Elsa-May asked.

"Yes, thanks, I have had dinner, but I'm always ready for dessert."

Crowley took a seat on a wooden chair next to Kelly's, while Kelly filled him in on everything that had happened, and about the fact that Cameron George had wanted his wife out of the way, according to his business partner.

Minutes later, when Ettie handed Crowley a bowl of apple pie and cream, she asked, "What do you make of what Detective Kelly just told you?"

"Yes, Crowley," Kelly said. "I'm interested in hearing your take on it."

"I'd say it would be crucial to find out who was

visiting Paula all the time, and why."

"The plates very nearly match the black car that was often seen in the street. And that car belongs to Cameron George, Nora's husband and Paula's old boss," Kelly said.

"But, Elizabeth has bad eyesight for distance," Elsa-May added.

Crowley twitched his nose and then rubbed it while clutching the dessert bowl in his other hand. "Would it be possible she saw two different cars—both black?"

"I suppose that's possible," Kelly said.

"Elizabeth only wrote the plate number down once. What if Paula's old boss only visited her once and that was the very time she recorded the plate number?"

"You think she had two visitors, both in black cars?" Kelly asked.

"I'm just thinking like a lawyer. I know Ettie and Elsa-May aren't very knowledgeable about makes and models of cars."

"That's true. One car looks like another to us.

And Elizabeth is nearly our age. I think it's the younger ones who know more about cars for some reason," Ettie said.

"So Paula's neighbour taking down the plate number is not going to convince anyone that the husband had anything to do with it?" Elsa-May asked Crowley.

"Yes, particularly when she has bad eyesight and didn't get the exact plate number. I know both of you say you suspect the husband, but you're going to need more than Paula's ex-boss visiting her. He's quite entitled to visit her."

Kelly stared at Ettie and Elsa-May. "Particularly when his description matches the description of other men that she knew."

Ettie sighed. "I feel so bad for the poor woman sitting in jail for something she didn't do."

"If she's not guilty she has nothing to worry about," Kelly said.

Elsa-May jutted out her bottom jaw. "We both know that's not so, Detective Kelly."

"I'll do my very best to uncover anything that

might be hidden," Kelly replied.

"Is there anything we might be missing, Ronald?" Ettie asked.

Crowley rubbed the side of his face. "The motive's not strong from Nora's point of view." He turned to Kelly. "So far you think that Nora did it because you found evidence, but what was her motive?"

Kelly frowned at Crowley. "Nora had a strong motive! Her husband had been having an affair with Paula over an extended period of time. We had an anonymous tip that Nora said she'd find out who her husband was having an affair with and kill her, but Nora denies that her husband had an affair. She knows nothing of that part of her husband's life, either that, or she's in denial."

"Anonymous tip?" Crowley asked before he took a mouthful of pie.

"Yes."

When Crowley had swallowed, he asked, "Is that it? Nora and Paula had never met before?"

"I forgot to mention that Paula was once

employed at Cameron George's furniture store," Kelly said.

"Cameron George?" Crowley asked. "Was he the same Cameron George who was on the force some years ago?"

Kelly nodded. "Many years ago."

"Yes, I vaguely remember him."

Ettie leaned forward. "What do you remember about him?"

"He left after an incident where someone was shot. There was an investigation. The details are hazy; it was too long ago."

"I'll look into that," Kelly said.

"Any other thoughts?" Elsa-May asked the retired detective.

"Yes, I'd be interested to hear them. It doesn't hurt to have a fresh perspective," Kelly said.

"If Nora George is innocent, who are your suspects?" Crowley asked.

"There's Obadiah Lapp who thinks Paula is his girlfriend."

Ettie protested, "It wouldn't be Obadiah. He's

just a simple boy."

Kelly looked at Ettie. "Crowley asked me, so I'm telling him how things are. As I was saying, Obadiah Lapp, Cameron George, Jason Peters who is Paula's brother, and possibly the business partner of Cameron George."

"Why the brother?" Crowley asked.

"He matches the description of the person seen visiting and he owns a black car very similar to Cameron George's car."

"But, do Paula's brother and Nora George know each other?"

Kelly wagged a finger at Crowley and smiled. "I see where you're going with this. I'll check into it."

Elsa-May and Ettie exchanged glances.

Ettie said to Crowley, "You think Paula's brother might have framed Nora? Paula's brother wouldn't have harmed his own sister."

"You'd have to find out more about their relationship and see if there was some kind of family feud. It stands to reason if Nora's innocent then she's obviously been framed. All we have to do is figure out who framed her."

"Her husband of course," Elsa-May said. "He had easy access to her car and her locket. He wanted his wife out of the way and what better way to do it than to get rid of two unwanted women in his life, both in one go?"

"Yes, Elsa-May, but we've got to look at these things from all angles," Kelly said before he turned to Crowley. "Anything else on your mind?"

"No. We just have to hope that the woman in the hospital recovers enough to tell us who attacked her."

"That's what we're hoping," Kelly said.

Chapter 10

The next morning, Ettie said to Elsa-May over breakfast, "You know, we should visit Paula's family and see what they knew about the relationship with her old boss."

"Cameron?"

"Yes. See if Paula mentioned anything to them."

"Do you think they'll talk to us if they think we're members of a cult?" Elsa-May asked.

"We have to try something."

"Okay, let's do it. How do we find out where they live?"

"The bishop gave Kelly their address. We don't want Kelly to know we're going there, so we'll call the bishop and get the address from him," Ettie said.

"You will, not 'we,'" Elsa-May said.

"It'd be better if you do it. You get along with him far better than me."

"Than I," Elsa-May corrected Ettie.

"Gut, you agree. So you'll ask him?"

Elsa-May breathed out heavily. "Okay."

* * *

Elsa-May arrived back at the house after calling the bishop. "They live in Kutztown."

"It sounds familiar. How far is that?"

"The bishop said about an hour by car. I guess it'll be longer by bus."

"Let's get to the bus depot as quick as we can."

"I thought you'd say that. I've already called for a taxi. I hope you're ready to go."

Ettie picked up a basket. "I've packed us some food for the trip."

"That wasn't necessary. I'm sure there'll be food on the way."

"I don't want to go hungry or find that I don't like the food that's available. I don't want to have to eat a bag of chips like we've so often had to do. This way we can have a proper meal."

Elsa-May nodded. *"Denke,* Ettie."

Snowy jumped up at Elsa-May and then pawed on her leg. "He knows we're going somewhere."

"He's a smart dog."

"You can't come with us, Snowy. I'll take you for an extra long walk when I get home." Elsa-May patted his head and he lay down on the floor.

A car horn beeped.

"That'll be our taxi."

When they told the taxi driver where they were off to, he made some inquiries and got them to the proper bus station. "There'll be a bus leaving here in half an hour."

"Thank you, you've been very helpful."

When they were heading into the bus station, Elsa-May said, "He was a friendly man, Ettie."

"He was and I think you were being a little too friendly with him."

"Jah, you're right. I was too friendly."

"You agree with me?"

"I do. I miss having a man around. A man to do all the little things that need repairing around the *haus."*

"We've got enough people who are willing to do things for us."

Elsa-May sighed. "It's not the same."

"Well, you're not getting married again at your age, and leaving me alone."

"*Nee,* I wouldn't marry again. Sometimes I miss what was. Do you remember how it was when you were the central person in everyone's lives? The hub of the *familye?*"

"*Jah,* when our *kinner* were young."

Elsa-May nodded. "What we said mattered then and all my *kinner* came to me with their problems and told me their hopes. Now, I'm not told anything."

"It's a cycle, Elsa-May. We need to enjoy this time of our lives too. Our parents probably felt just the same as we're feeling now."

"I know, but I just got to thinking how it used to be. Now our *kinner* hardly visit us."

"That's because we live so close we see them all the time at the meetings."

"I'm just thinking…"

"Well, don't think! All this emotion just from talking to the taxi driver?"

Elsa-May remained silent and Ettie could see that her sister was stuck in this loop of melancholy thoughts. "We need to keep busy, Elsa-May. Remember when we were wondering if Paula had a dark past?"

Elsa-May nodded.

"We have to ask her family the right questions."

"Do you think we should've let them know we were coming?"

"Nee, because they might have told us not to bother."

"Jah, good point. We'll have to hope that they're home."

* * *

"Is this it?" Ettie looked up at Paula's parents' home as the taxi pulled up in the street.

"This is the address I got from the bishop."

"It doesn't look very grand. I thought the family

123

was wealthy."

The taxi driver, overhearing Ettie, said, "This is one of the better streets in these parts."

"I see. Thank you," Ettie said. "How much do we owe you?" she asked the driver.

While Ettie was paying the driver, Elsa-May tugged on her sleeve.

"Ettie, look! There's someone coming out of the house. That could be the brother. Come on."

"I'm coming. You go on ahead."

Ettie finished paying the driver and then caught up with Elsa-May who was striding toward the young man. The man clicked a remote control and the lights of a nearby car lit up.

When he saw them approach, he stood still. "Can I help you?"

"We're friends of Paula and we've come to talk to her family. Would you be a family member?"

"I'm her brother, Jason. My parents aren't home, and that's just as well because you wouldn't get a very good response from them. Have you come to ask how Paula is?"

"We were told that her condition hasn't changed," Ettie said.

"I know. I just phoned the hospital and was told the same."

"We'd just like to ask you some questions if we could."

"Questions about my sister?"

"Yes."

"Go right ahead."

"This is quite a delicate matter. Do you know why your sister left the furniture store where she was working before she joined our community?"

"I do and by the sounds of it, you do too."

Ettie and Elsa-May looked at each other.

"My sister was strung along for years by that man saying he was going to leave his wife. He never did. And then he took on a female business partner, and my sister was pushed to one side. How do you think she felt about that?"

"Not very good, I would imagine," Ettie said, feeling sorry for Paula wasting years on the wrong man.

"That's when she left the store, when the business partner came to work there?" Elsa-May asked.

"I talked her into leaving. I told her she couldn't wait around forever. She'd already wasted enough of her time on him. He's probably giving the business partner the same line about leaving his wife."

"Possibly," Ettie said.

"I went to see him myself and told him what I thought of him."

"What happened," Elsa-May asked.

"I told him my sister was considering telling his wife and telling his new business partner about the relationship they'd had."

"Did Paula tell anyone about their relationship?" Elsa-May asked.

"No and I'd wager Cameron George knew Paula would never talk. She's too much of a peaceful person who wouldn't like to make waves. Anyway, he just laughed in my face."

"Yes, she seems a quiet person," Ettie said.

"She joined the Amish because she'd lost

faith—I think. She was looking for something to have faith in," he said. "Now we've lost her to the Amish."

Elsa-May said, "I'm sorry you feel that way, but Paula would feel she was lost but now she's been found."

He tossed his dark hair back and laughed. "I've heard it all before. My parents made us go to church when we were younger and I never bought into it, but my sister is more gullible than I am. She needed a crutch, and then she ran into some Amish people somewhere along the way when she was feeling down. They must've recruited her."

"That's not our way," Ettie said with a frown.

"She's Amish now, and she had to come by that decision somehow. I remember her telling me about a family she met."

"The Lapp family?" Elsa-May asked.

"Yes, I think that's what their names were."

"She lived with the Lapps before she moved into her own house. Have you visited her since she joined us?"

"I didn't visit her when she was staying with that Amish family. I went to see her once or twice after she'd bought the house."

"What was it, once, or was it twice?" Elsa-May asked.

Ettie looked at her sister and wished that she'd gone alone to talk with Paula's family. Questions like that would definitely get anyone off track.

The brother didn't seem fazed by Elsa-May's blunt tone. "I believe it was twice. Once when she first moved in, and then a couple of months after that. I called in to see if she was okay."

"So that was the last time you saw her?" Elsa-May asked.

He tipped his head to one side. "How are you trying to help my sister?"

"We're trying to find out who did this to her."

Elsa-May added, "Your answers have been a big help so far."

"I'll do whatever I can to help. I don't know why they aren't letting family in to see Paula, though, especially since she might not make it."

"They aren't letting anyone see her," Ettie said, "When you visited her, did she say anything about having an enemy or someone she'd upset?"

"The only person she would've upset would be Cameron George."

"What did she do to upset him?"

"Just what I told you." He glanced at his watch. "I'll have to go soon. It was my mistake telling him that she was thinking of telling his wife. I just wanted to give him a fright—nothing more."

"You think it was Cameron George who hurt her?"

"I absolutely do. And I hear his wife's locked up for it and he's free."

"Did you tell the police all you told us?"

"I was here when the police came to talk with my parents. They didn't take the line of questioning down the road that you have. So I didn't mention anything. If my sister doesn't pull through, that'll be a different story. I'll find out myself who did this to her and make them pay."

"Is there anything else you need to tell us?" Ettie

asked.

He shook his head. "Not right now. I can't think of anything."

"You've been very helpful."

"Did you know my sister very well?"

"We did. We were going to see her the very morning that all this dreadful business happened. We hadn't seen her in a while."

Ettie nodded. "We were dreadfully shocked when we heard the news."

"I imagine it would've been shocking." He glanced at his watch again. "If you ladies will excuse me, I'm running late for a meeting."

"Thank you once again. You've been very helpful."

"Bye now," Ettie said.

They stood on the edge of the street watching Paula's brother drive away in a black car.

"That's another black car, Ettie."

"And another tall man with dark hair. His number plate is nothing like the one Elizabeth gave to Kelly, though."

"What do you think about his story?" Elsa-May asked.

"What did you think?"

"Do you believe him?"

"Maybe. He seemed quite believable," Ettie said.

"I wonder if he might have had some reasons to want his sister out of the way."

"Like what?" Ettie asked.

"It occurred to me that he didn't want us to speak with his parents. He seemed to act relieved that they're not home. You know, how he spoke about them in a negative way as if they would be hostile with us."

"*Jah,* but that goes along with what the detective said about them saying that we were a cult."

"I suppose so, but I don't want to be turned off from talking to them."

"Are you suggesting we should wait for them to come home?"

Elsa-May nodded. "That might be a good idea."

"What? Do you want to wait for them to come

home? With no food and no water?"

"Don't be so dramatic, Ettie."

"I'm not being dramatic. You were the one who ate all the food I brought with us. No wonder you're not hungry."

"We'll wait here for an hour and then if they haven't shown up we'll go and get something to eat somewhere and then come back."

Ettie smiled. "That sounds like a good idea."

Ettie and Elsa-May found a seat at a nearby bus stop where they had a good view of the comings and goings at the house.

They only had to wait half an hour before a white sedan pulled into the driveway and into the garage. As soon as the car was inside, the doors closed.

Elsa-May slapped Ettie on the shoulder as she said, "Come on; that'll be them. Let's go."

"Give an old girl a minute," Ettie said before she stood up. Elsa-May hadn't waited, and Ettie made spritely strides to catch up with her at the bottom of the driveway.

"I'll go knock on the door," Elsa-May said.

"I'm right behind you," Ettie said in a quiet voice.

An elderly man opened the door.

"Would you be Paula Peters' father?" Elsa-May asked.

"Yes."

"I'm a friend of hers."

"Have you heard what happened to her?" he asked as he looked from Ettie to Elsa-May.

"Yes, that's why we're here."

"Would you like to come in?" he asked.

"Yes, thank you, if you don't mind."

"If I minded I wouldn't have asked," he said with a smile. "Come through and I'll call my wife." The man yelled out to his wife.

He showed them through to the sitting room.

Ettie wasn't expecting such a good response from him and hoped that his wife would be just as nice. While they were waiting for Paula's mother, Ettie and Elsa-May introduced themselves.

"There you are," he said when his wife walked into the room. "These ladies know Paula."

She opened her mouth as though she was a little surprised and then she sat down.

After the introductions were over, Elsa-May said, "We're here to ask you a couple of questions."

Ettie added, "Only because we want to know who harmed Paula."

"We told the police everything we know." Mr. Peters said.

"There might be something that you didn't think was relevant," Ettie said.

Elsa-May asked, "What did you know about the furniture store where Paula worked?"

Paula's mother said, "You know about the affair?"

Ettie and Elsa-May nodded.

"We've heard some talk that there was an affair and that she was dumped for the new business partner," Ettie said.

Elsa-May stared at Ettie, "There's no need to put it quite so brutally."

"Well that's how I heard it happened," Ettie said. She turned to Paula's parents. "I'm sorry, if I've said something wrong."

"Don't be sorry," Paula's mother said, "It seems that's just what happened even though it took place well over a year ago."

"The police told us that Cameron George's wife is accused of assaulting Paula. It seems she found out that Paula was having an affair with her husband," Mr. Peters said.

"That's what they think," Elsa-May said.

Mr. Peters narrowed his eyes. "But you think something different? You think Cameron George did this to her?"

"Is that what you think?" Mrs. Peters asked.

"We don't know. Do you know if Cameron George ever gave Paula a locket?"

"She wouldn't have told us if he had. She kept the whole thing secret until she told us she was joining you people."

"Paula gave us a few surprises that day. She told us she didn't even want us to name her in our wills."

Mr. Peters continued, "She said her inheritance

was not an earthly one, but a heavenly one. I don't have a lot, but I worked hard so I have something to leave both my son and my daughter. It hurt me when she turned her back like that."

Mrs. Peters began to cry. "They won't even let us see her, even though she might not make it."

Mr. Peters put his arm around his wife. "We've just come from the hospital. They've run all the tests they can, and they won't know more until she wakes up."

"Do you know anybody who would want to harm Paula?" Ettie asked. "Besides the Georges?"

While Mrs. Peters shook her head, Mr. Peters said, "No!"

"I'd reckon it was something to do with Cameron George," Mr. Peters said.

Ettie and Elsa-May walked out of the house half an hour later.

"We didn't learn much," Ettie said.

"Not much. Do you think they had more information they were keeping to themselves?"

"I don't think so. I think they would've told us."

"I can't help thinking we're missing something."

"*Jah* we are. We're missing knowing who attacked her."

"You know what I mean, Ettie."

"I wonder if she'd been threatened before. And if she had been threatened, who would she have told about it?"

"Would she have gone to the bishop?"

Elsa-May shook her head. "The bishop didn't know anything about it. He would've said something to the detective, wouldn't he?"

"You know him better than I do. What do you think?"

"With something as important as this, I do think that he would've mentioned it."

"So we can take it that the bishop doesn't know?" Ettie asked.

Elsa-May nodded. "Now, who were Paula's closest friends in the community?"

"She seemed to be very close with Mrs. Lapp."

"*Ach nee!* We don't have to go back there and

talk to them again, do we?"

"The last time we were there was the only time that they know we visited them because the first time they weren't home. We only spoke to Obadiah and he probably didn't tell them we had visited. He doesn't talk much even to his parents."

"That's true. So how do we approach this?"

"Let's figure something out on the bus back home."

Chapter 11

Ettie and Elsa-May figured out that if cake had worked in getting Elizabeth to talk, it might also work on Mrs. Lapp.

They went to a cake shop as soon as they got off the bus.

Elsa-May walked in first and right away pointed at a passionfruit sponge with thick icing. "That looks like a nice one."

"You're just saying that because of the thick icing."

Elsa-May chuckled. "I do have a sweet tooth and there's nothing wrong with that."

"Nothing wrong with it unless you're trying to lose weight."

"I've already lost some," Elsa-May protested.

Ettie frowned at Elsa-May and looked her up and down. How she thought she'd lost weight, Ettie didn't know. She certainly looked the same size, and her clothes didn't look any looser, but Ettie wasn't going to tell her that.

"Do you think she'd like the passionfruit one, or the chocolate cake?"

"I prefer the chocolate cake myself, but I think she might prefer the passionfruit sponge."

Somehow Ettie doubted that. How could her sister possibly know what kind of cake Mrs. Lapp liked—they weren't that close with her.

"Can I help you there?"

Ettie looked up at the sales assistant. "I'll take the passionfruit sponge please."

Elsa-May smiled and rubbed her sister's shoulder. "A great, good choice, Ettie. I'm sure she'll like that one."

"Would you like that in a box?" the assistant asked.

"Yes, please, a box would help us carry it better. A box is a lot better than putting the cake on a plate and then in a paper bag."

Elsa-May leaned in and whispered to Ettie, "A yes or no was all that was required."

Ettie whispered back, "I'm just being nice to the

poor girl. She looks tired and I think she's had a hard day."

"Haven't we all?" Elsa-May said.

* * *

"How nice of you to visit me again."

"And we've brought cake," Elsa-May said.

"Jah, your favourite passionfruit cake," Ettie added.

"Wunderbaar!" Once they were all inside, Mrs. Lapp said, "Come through to the kitchen. Have you any news of Paula?"

"Nee. We were wondering if you'd heard anything."

Ettie set the cakebox on the counter, and they all sat down at the kitchen table.

Diane Lapp shook her head. *"Nee.* We only went to the hospital the one time, and we weren't allowed to see her. That policeman came again today to speak to Obadiah."

"The detective—the one that came when Elsa-

May and I were here?"

She nodded. "That's the one. He didn't look like he was going to give up so I let him ask Obadiah some questions. I didn't know what else to do because Boris wasn't home."

"Did you stay with Obadiah?" Elsa-May asked.

"Yes, I did because I knew Boris would've wanted me to stay with him. I hope Boris won't be angry with me when he gets home."

"What did he ask him?"

"Nothing much. Did he know how to drive a car, how well he knew Paula, had he ever been to Paula's house. That's some of the questions I can remember."

"What did Obadiah say?"

"He answered him honestly and I think the detective was satisfied with his answers."

"Did the detective say anything else?"

"Let me put the pot on to boil while I think about it." She filled the pot with water and placed it on the stove. "Will you open the cake box for me, Ettie? While I fix the tea?"

"Of course." Ettie busied herself at the counter, cutting the cake and serving it onto small plates.

When Diane Lapp sat back down, she said, "I can't think that he said too much else. He showed Obadiah some photos and asked him if he recognized the people, then he told him some names and asked if he knew them." She shook her head. "Don't ask me what names; I wouldn't remember now, as they weren't people I know and neither did Obadiah."

"I hope that wasn't too upsetting for Obadiah."

"He didn't seem to mind at all."

"Can Obadiah drive a car?" Elsa-May asked.

"He's never been on *rumspringa* and he wouldn't be able to go. He can't look after himself. I wouldn't be able to trust him to live on his own, or with others."

"Was Paula ever frightened of anyone that you know of?"

Diane shook her head. "An *Englischer?*"

"*Jah.*"

"*Nee,* she never mentioned anything of the

kind."

Ettie stored it in her brain for later that Obadiah's mother evaded the question about whether Obadiah could drive a car. "You two were close, weren't you?" Ettie asked.

"Quite close." Diane nodded. "We never spoke about her past life, though, from before she arrived here. Well, she did in little bits and pieces, but only generally. She never gave me details and I didn't ask."

"What kind of things?" Elsa-May asked.

"She mentioned she'd had many disappointments in her life." Diane stood. "Let's have some of this lovely cake."

"Denke, that would be *wunderbaar,"* Elsa-May said with a huge grin.

"We weren't sure what cake you like best. It was either this one or a chocolate cake," Ettie said.

"I like either. Now, tea or *kaffe?"*

"Tea for both of us, please," Elsa-May said.

Chapter 12

Right after they left Diane Lapp's house, Ettie and Elsa-May headed to the police station. They had to find out why the detective would speak with Obadiah at all since last time they spoke with Kelly, he'd seemed certain the guilty party was either Cameron George or his wife, Nora.

"What possible reason would you have to want to speak with Obadiah when you've got so much evidence against Cameron George?" Ettie asked when she and Elsa-May sat opposite him in his office.

"That's none of your business."

"It became my business when you asked for my help," Ettie said firmly.

He sighed heavily. "I can't put my investigation at risk by telling you."

"You won't be winning yourself any friends once word gets around that you deliberately went to the Lapps' house when Mr. Lapp wasn't home and forced Mrs. Lapp to allow you to speak with Obadiah."

Detective Kelly scowled. "That's not how it happened."

"Isn't it?" Elsa-May asked. "That's the way we heard it."

Ettie said, "If it wasn't, that's what everyone will think. Why do you ask for my help at all?"

"You know most of the people in your community slam the door in my face. Not literally, but you know what I mean."

"Why couldn't you tell us what you wanted to find out from Obadiah?"

"Last time I checked you weren't a member of the force. Anything you asked him wouldn't be on record."

"What was so important? How can he possibly be involved in any of this? None of his prints were found in Paula's house," Ettie said.

The detective remained silent and lowered his head.

"What? They found his prints in Paula's house?"

Ettie asked.

He sighed. "I wasn't going to tell you, but yes. They found many of his prints in the house."

Elsa-May asked, "But not on the weapon or the locket?"

"No, as I said, the only prints on the locket and the tire iron were Nora's."

"Did he say what he was doing inside Paula's house?"

"He admitted to going there a week or so ago. Paula wasn't home, so he walked inside. After waiting, he left and went home. Now, it's possible that all his prints that were found in the house were left on that occasion."

Ettie and Elsa-May looked at each other. Mrs. Lapp hadn't mentioned any of that to them.

"Elizabeth mustn't have seen him," Elsa-May said. "But she didn't mention anything to us. She said she's home most of the time."

"Not many people are home all the time, or by their windows all day. Obadiah said he couldn't drive a car, but I found out that's not true. I see many Amish boys in cars."

"Only on their *rumspringa,*" Ettie informed him.

"With ten older brothers, or however many he has, I'm certain most of them would've gone on *rumspringa* and brought cars back home," Kelly said.

"Some do when they visit their parents, but I think you're reading too much into things."

"I think the only thing he's guilty of is going into someone's home when they weren't about, but we do that all the time if we know the people well enough," Elsa-May said. "We generally don't lock our doors."

"Last time we spoke with you, you were confident you had the guilty party behind bars already."

He sighed. "I threw out a hint, but you didn't take it. I might as well tell you that we had Obadiah's prints already in the system."

Ettie gasped. "I didn't even put two and two together."

"Neither did I. Has be been arrested previously, then?" Elsa-May asked.

Kelly nodded. "And he lied to me, which makes me think if he lies about one thing he'll think nothing of lying about another."

"What was he arrested for?"

"Driving unlicensed, speeding, and driving under the influence of alcohol. He had a court appearance, and according to our records, it was Paula Peters who stood up for him in court and explained his situation. He didn't get jail time, he got a stern warning and a fine."

Ettie's fingertips flew to her mouth. Mrs. Lapp hadn't mentioned any of that to them. And, more than that, she and her husband had made it seem as though Obadiah barely spoke to Paula and hardly knew her. Now Ettie knew that was not the case— unless Diane Lapp was totally unaware of the situation.

"Mrs. Lapp told us none of that," Elsa-May said.

"She was protecting her son. That's why Mr. Lapp didn't want him to speak with us. He knew his son had that past run-in with us."

"So, knowing that Obadiah knew Paula better

149

than any of us thought, do you think he played any part in her attack?" Ettie asked.

"I'm just putting all the pieces of the puzzle together. I had to find out why his prints were in her house and I wanted to hear it from him."

"Did you know all this the first time you came to the Lapp's house?"

"I can't tell you that, Mrs. Smith."

"Why not?"

"Let's just say I've known since we got all the results of the prints back."

"What about fingerprints of Cameron George? Were any of his prints found at the house?"

"Yes, I think I told you that already. When I first identified him from the photo in the locket and went to his furniture store, I had a long talk with him. He told me the situation between Paula and himself and that he'd visited Paula recently to make certain she was doing okay. He was very distressed to find out she was harmed."

"He must be a good actor," Elsa-May said.

"And a quick thinker," Ettie added.

"What do you mean?" Kelly asked.

"That was quick thinking to tell you he'd visited Paula."

"You two certainly have it in for this man."

Ettie turned down her lips and wondered if she were being influenced by Cameron George's behaviour.

"Would you let us talk with Nora again?" Elsa-May asked.

"No! I can't. I couldn't if I wanted to. She was removed to another prison today where she'll await trial."

"The big prison?" Ettie asked.

"Yes, the state prison. She'll have to get used to it. It might be her new home for many years."

"Are you that certain she's guilty?" Ettie asked.

"That's up to the courts to decide."

"What about the taxi driver you were going to question. The one who said he took a woman to Paula's street."

"We had no luck with the taxi driver. He picked up the woman late at night, but he said he wouldn't

151

be able to identify her and she didn't book the taxi by phone."

"So there's no record of her?"

"That's right. She paid by cash, he remembers that much and he didn't record it on his books."

"And he told you that?" Ettie asked.

"I'm not the IRS." Detective Kelly said.

"So that doesn't give us any information. Does he remember exactly where he picked her up and what time?"

Kelly shook his head. "I showed him a photograph of Nora George and he said it might have been her but he couldn't say one hundred percent whether it was her or not."

"Was it on the same night that Paula was attacked?"

"He says he was certain it was the same night."

Ettie breathed out heavily.

"If you'll excuse me I've got a few things to check on."

Chapter 13

"Why don't we ask Crowley if he'll go and talk with Nora? I'm certain she'll be allowed visitors. Crowley should know all about how to get in and see her."

"Why would he do that?"

"Because you'll ask him."

Ettie pouted. "I suppose he would know all the things to ask her. It's probably a good idea to ask him to do it."

"I won't argue with you."

"I admit it was a good idea. Crowley respects the force of the law and that's why he'll most likely try to help."

"Let's go home and call from there."

They asked the taxi driver to stop just down the road from the house, and Ettie called Crowley from the phone in the shanty. She knew Crowley's cell phone number by heart.

He answered on the third beep. "Detective

Crowley, is that you?"

"Ettie?"

"Yes."

"I told you, call me Ronald."

Ettie giggled. "Yes, I forgot."

"What is it?"

"Elsa-May and I were wondering if you might visit Nora George."

"Isn't she in jail?"

"That's the one."

"What does Kelly say?" Crowley inquired.

"Kelly has doubts now that she did it, but I guess he's not in a position to work too hard to get her out. Unless other evidence comes out, he'll probably leave it to the courts to decide. That's what he's always saying—*let the courts decide.*"

"Is she still in the station's lock up?"

"No, she's been removed to a different jail, but I don't know where. Is there more than one she could've gone to?"

"Yes, there's more than one. I'll make a few calls and find out where she is. What would you like me to find out?"

"You'll do it?"

"I don't know yet. You'll have to tell me a little more first. Convince me."

Ettie told Crowley everything she knew and all that she and Elsa-May suspected. Most of it, he already knew from when they'd spoken to him before.

"Okay leave it with me," Crowley said.

"You'll do it?"

"Yes. I'll come to see you after I speak with her."

"Thank you, Cr... Ronald. I hate to see the poor woman in jail for something she didn't do"

"Well, if you want me to help, you'll need to get off the phone so I can make some calls." He chuckled.

"Oh. Yes, right away." Ettie replaced the receiver.

"Ettie, you didn't say goodbye to him."

"He said he needed to make calls."

"Come on, let's get back home and I'll take Snowy for a walk."

It was after dinner when the sisters got a surprise visit from the retired detective, Crowley.

"Ronald!" Elsa-May said when she opened the door.

"I have some news."

"Come inside and take a seat."

When he walked inside, Ettie pushed herself up from her couch. "Have you been to see Nora already?"

"I have." Crowley sat on a wooden chair opposite Ettie, and Ettie and Elsa-May sat down in their usual spots. "Nora's very frightened. She doesn't belong in a place like that. I put it to her that her husband framed her. She admitted that it made sense, but she said that would be the worst thing in the world she could think of."

"Did you bring up her husband's affairs?"

"Yes. She finally admitted she knew about his affairs, but blamed herself for not being a good enough wife."

"That's interesting that she knew about them. Did she know he'd had more than one?" Ettie asked.

"I referred to them as 'affairs' and she didn't correct me. I can't see that she has enough venom in her to kill anyone," he said.

"Then you believe us that she's not guilty?" Elsa-May asked.

"Yes, but unless her husband confesses, I can't see her getting off the hook."

"Hmm, I wonder, what would it take for him to confess?" Ettie said.

"Nothing, I'd say. He'll know what he'll be facing if he confesses. He wouldn't have gone to all the trouble to frame her and then confess to it. This is what he wanted."

"Am I right to say that if he confesses now, his charges will be less than if the police keep investigating and then arrest him?" Ettie asked.

"What Ettie means is, if he steps forward now, will things be easier for him? Will he be able to cut a deal?" Elsa-May asked.

"I don't know if there's any deal for him to be able to make in this scenario, but you're right about things maybe going easier for him if he confesses."

Ettie said, "All we have to do is let him know all the evidence Kelly has against him, and then if he has any sense he'd come forward before Kelly arrests him."

"Good luck with that," Crowley said.

"What do you mean?" Elsa-May asked.

"Kelly has strong evidence on the wife. All the husband did was have affairs and the only thing that points to him was the Internet search which could've been easily performed by Nora herself."

"His laptop was password protected," Elsa-May pointed out.

"The prosecution will say that she might have known his password. She is his wife and knows the way he thinks. She could've figure it out."

Ettie fiddled with the strings of her prayer *kapp*. "What evidence is there that he did it, Elsa-May?"

"There isn't any, except that he benefits from getting Paula out of the way and his wife out of the way. There's the car that has a similar plate number. Then there are his prints that were in the house, but he covered himself there."

"Yes, by admitting to visiting her."

"You're going to need something more than that," Crowley said.

"What else did Nora tell you?" Ettie asked him.

"Nothing much besides the fact that there is the possibility that her husband framed her. She wouldn't hear of it—she seems very sweet and unassuming. Although, she is worried that the lawyer Cameron got for her isn't good. She's also concerned that her husband has made no effort to visit her. She told me her husband isn't visiting her because he's ashamed of her because he thinks she's guilty."

"Who does *she* suspect did it, then?" Elsa-May asked.

He shook his head. "She doesn't know."

"If you believe us, could you have a talk with Detective Kelly?"

Crowley chuckled. "It won't make a difference—it's evidence we need. What you or I think, or even what Kelly thinks, won't affect anything."

"Did you look into the accidental shooting

you mentioned? The one that Cameron George was involved in years ago when he was a police officer?" Ettie asked.

"Yes. I should hear back about that soon. I've got a friend looking into that for me."

"Good!" Elsa-May said.

"Ronald, have you thought any more about becoming a private detective like you mentioned before?"

He rubbed his chin. "I'm still thinking about it, Ettie—still thinking."

Chapter 14

When Ettie and Elsa-May woke the next morning they decided to visit Paula in the hospital.

"What makes you think they'll allow us in when not even her parents have been allowed to see her?"

"I don't know, Elsa-May, but we have to do something and this just feels right."

"She's in Ward B room 3, but she's not allowed visitors," the nurse behind the front desk said.

"She isn't?"

The nurse shook her head. "I'm sorry."

"That's okay. I might sit here and rest a while."

The nurse looked back down at the work in front of her.

Ettie and Elsa-May sat for some time and when the nurse left her station, and another nurse took over, Ettie said, "Let's go."

"I'm right behind you."

"Ward B is on the second floor," Elsa-May said

when she pushed the button on the elevator.

"When we get out we must look like we know where we're going so no one stops us."

"Okay," Elsa-May agreed.

When the doors opened, both ladies headed right. Before long they were following signs to ward B and when they turned a corner, they saw an officer seated outside a door. They knew it was the door of Paula Peters' room. They walked up to him.

"Are you ladies trying to see Paula Peters?"

"We were hoping to," Ettie said.

"She's a member of our community and we're here to pray for her," Elsa-May added.

"I'm sorry, but like I tell that lady who comes here every day, no one's allowed in."

"Did you say a lady visits her every day?"

"Every single day."

"What does she look like?"

"She's a tall slender woman with short black hair, kind of cropped off at the chin. She says she's a friend of Paula."

"Did she tell you her name?" Ettie asked

knowing the description matched Cameron's business partner.

"No."

"Can't we go and stand by her?" Elsa-May said.

"You can come into the room too," Ettie said.

He shook his head. "I've got my orders. There are only two nurses allowed in and the two doctors that have been attending her. Other than those four people, no one is allowed in."

"Have you been here every day?" Ettie asked.

"Yes. I've been doing the days and two other officers split the nights." The officer smiled.

"We'll have to wait until she wakes up then."

"That would be best."

They turned to walk back to the elevator. "Ettie, we'll have to go and tell the detective that the woman has been trying to get in to see Paula."

"*Jah,* we will. It sounds like it's Cameron George's business partner from the description. There can't be too many women around here with black cropped hair."

As they approached the station to speak with the

detective, they saw Cameron George's business partner, Casey Campbell, walking down the front steps.

"Look! She's right there. I wonder what she was doing at the police station," Ettie said.

"Possibly Kelly had her in for questioning and it's about time too."

They hurried inside the station, spoke to the officer at the front desk, and then sat and waited for Detective Kelly. It was some time before he came out.

Instead of bringing them into his office, he crouched down in front of them. "I'm sorry, I'm strapped for time. We've just been blown away. Casey Campbell told us that Cameron George admitted to her that he framed his wife—tried to frame her for murder. We're in the midst of getting a warrant for his arrest."

"He told her that?" Ettie asked.

"Yes, and she was horrified. But Casey has agreed to testify against him. Not only that, but we did some checking into the accident that Crowley mentioned the other night."

"The gun accident where someone was killed when Cameron George was a police officer?"

"Yes. They let him off—gave him the benefit of the doubt, but there was no evidence that he didn't kill a fellow officer. He left the force soon after."

"Does that mean you'll set Nora George free?" Elsa-May asked.

"Yes. Casey said Cameron told her last night, and she came in to tell us as soon as she could."

"Isn't that what we've been saying all along?" Ettie asked him.

"I know. I know, but until we had a witness or evidence, our hands were tied." He stood up. "We'll just have to hope that Paula pulls through."

"Although, I had started to wonder if it were Casey Campbell who was the guilty party." Ettie pushed herself to her feet. "We were just at the hospital. A woman fitting Casey's description has gone there every day trying to get in to see Paula."

He stared at Ettie. "According to my officers, there have been quite a few people who've tried to talk their ways into see her. They do know each other, Casey and Paula. They both worked together at the furniture store." He looked at the two of them. "Is that all?"

"That's all we came to tell you."

Elsa-May stood up. "When Paula wakes, she'll be able to say who did this to her."

"That's what we're hoping, as long as she remembers and hasn't suffered any permanent brain damage. Now, if you'll excuse me, I've got a million things to do. I need to split myself into three people to get everything done. I'll talk to you ladies later." Detective Kelly turned and walked away leaving Ettie and Elsa-May staring after him.

"What do you make of it all, Ettie?"

Ettie sat back down and Elsa-May sat down next to her.

"It bothers me that the woman visited Paula. Why would she?"

"My thoughts exactly. They can't have been friendly, either, if they both had wanted the same man."

"They've had an officer on the door because the person who did this to her might come and try to finish her off," Elsa-May said.

"Are you thinking Casey Campbell did it?"

"Do you?"

"It's possible," Ettie said. "But why would Casey say Cameron had confessed to her?"

"As a payback. She must have been mad that she'd been involved with him for a whole year and then he still hadn't left his wife."

"So she framed Nora, to get his wife out of the way?"

"*Jah,* and what better victim than someone else who once had an affair with Cameron? Especially if she found out Cameron was still visiting Paula. He must've still had feelings for Paula in some way or another."

"That wouldn't have gone down well with Casey Campbell if she'd found out about that," Ettie said.

"It might have been Casey who made that search on his computer. Since she was his business partner, she might have known his password."

Ettie pressed her lips together. "Do you think we should tell Detective Kelly?"

Elsa-May shook her head. "He doesn't like to look like a fool, and if we're right, that's exactly what he'll look like. First he arrests Nora, now he's going to arrest Cameron, but what if we're right and it was Casey all the way along?"

"You know what he's like about us interfering."

"He'll thank us if we're right, though," Elsa-May said.

"But are we?"

"Surely Kelly will figure it all out sooner or later. He'll bring Cameron in and question him."

"He said he was going to arrest him and set Nora free."

"*Jah,* but when he brings him in under arrest, he'll have to question him and Cameron will know that Casey Campbell either lied about him or betrayed his confidence. If he's innocent he won't confess and he'll tell Kelly that Casey lied."

"Kelly might not believe him."

"Think about it. If Cameron were guilty and his

mistress had sold him out, that would be his time to confess. Remember when we talked about it before? It'd be better for him to confess."

"So, we don't tell Kelly, is that what you're saying?"

"Jah. We don't tell him our suspicions because we have no evidence."

"Let's go and find some, then."

"Okay."

"Are you still waiting on Detective Kelly?"

Ettie and Elsa-May looked up to see an officer.

"No, we're on our way out. We've already spoken with him."

The officer smiled, and nodded before he continued on his way.

On the way down the front steps of the station, Elsa-May asked, "How are we going to find evidence that Casey Campbell did it?"

"I thought you had an idea," Ettie said.

"I don't."

"You usually do."

"Well, this time I've drawn a blank. We don't

even know where she lives."

"A phone call to Ava will remedy that," Elsa-May said.

"I know, but we don't even have a plan."

"One step at a time. We'll find a phone, call Ava, then she can call her friend at the DMV and then we'll have her address in no time. Then we'll figure out what to do."

Ettie nodded. "There's a phone up this way."

Half an hour later, Ettie and Elsa-May had Casey Campbell's address in their hands.

"We don't know anything about this woman."

"Ava said to call her again this afternoon. She's finding out what she can about her."

"Gut!"

"What good will following her do?"

"I don't know, but we have to do something."

Not long after they got Casey Campbell's address, they had a taxi drive past her house.

"She doesn't appear to be home."

"How can you tell?" Ettie asked.

"It's daytime, wouldn't she be at work?"

"I guess she would be." Ettie leaned over and gave the taxi driver the address of George's furniture store.

When the taxi stopped at the store, Elsa-May opened the door, but Ettie yelled out, "No!"

"What, Ettie?"

Ettie ordered the driver to take them back to the station. "I've got it all figured out, Elsa-May. I've got to see Detective Kelly urgently."

Chapter 15

A day later, Ettie was sitting in Paula's hospital room behind a screen when she heard the door open. Ettie quietly stood up and peered through a crack in the screen. It was Nora George. Nora walked over to Paula's bedside and from her bag she pulled a syringe.

"Stop right there!" Ettie said.

Nora swung around while pushing the syringe back into her bag. "It's you."

"Yes, it is."

"I was just coming to see how she's doing."

"She woke up earlier and said you were the one who attacked her."

"She did? Then why haven't the police come to get me?"

"Admit it. You did it and tried to make it look like your husband framed you."

Nora glanced down at Paula and then slowly put her hand into her bag. "Now why do you think that?"

"I know it's the truth. I admire how clever you are."

Nora chuckled. "It was a good plan and it worked, but I'm afraid you should've kept your mouth shut because now I'm going to have to kill you and then I'll finish her off." She lunged forward and grabbed Ettie.

"Wait! Before you kill me, tell me how you did it. You framed your husband to look like he was framing you?

She laughed. "Clever, don't you think?"

"No! I figured it out, so it won't be long before the police figure it out, too."

"Ha! That bumbling detective? I doubt he'd have the brains to work it out."

"I have to admire you for planning such a clever murder—except for the part that the victim wasn't dead when you left her.

Ettie jerked out of Nora's grasp and backed away from her. "What's in the syringe?"

"Insulin."

"You're going to kill me with insulin?"

"Yes. They won't suspect a thing. Might not even do an autopsy because you're so old."

"My sister wouldn't let them do an autopsy; neither would my children if they have a choice."

"Your sister. That's where I'll be heading next."

"Won't that be a little too suspicious if my sister and I both die?"

"No! Not at her age."

"Why did you do it? Your husband's affair with Paula ended over a year ago."

"I've got a long memory. Once they find my husband guilty of Paula's murder, and they *will* find him guilty, then I'll deal with his other mistress."

"Casey Campbell?"

Nora laughed. "No. She helped me plan this whole thing."

Ettie inquired, "Who then?"

"There was another."

"You mean you'll kill her, too, like you tried to kill Paula?"

"Just like I'm going to kill you now."

Kelly stepped out from the bathroom. "I've got all I need, Mrs. Smith." He held a tape in his hand. Nora made a lunge for the tape, and two uniformed officers rushed out from behind Kelly and slapped Nora in handcuffs.

"This was a trap?" She turned as far as she was able and stared at Ettie.

Ettie raised her eyebrows. "It wouldn't have been a trap if you'd had nothing to hide."

"I hope she dies." Nora nodded to Paula.

"I won't," Paula said as she opened her eyes.

Detective Kelly said, "Paula regained consciousness this morning and told us everything."

"Just like I told you," Ettie said.

"I was making it all up," Nora said.

"And that's not insulin in that syringe?" Kelly asked.

"I found it on my way into the hospital. I don't know what's in it."

"Tell it to a jury," Kelly said as he led Nora George out the door.

Ettie stood and made her way over to Paula.

"How are you feeling after all that?"

"I'm fine, Ettie. I'm just sorry I've put everyone through all of this."

"We're happy you've recovered and you were able to tell the police everything. Your parents are on their way to see you."

"The community are my *familye* now."

"I know that, but they were terribly worried about you. Elsa-May and I visited them and spoke with them."

"*Denke.* Will you stay with me for a while, Ettie? I don't want to be alone."

"Of course I will, for however long you want."

"The doctor said he wants to run some tests on me this afternoon. All I want to do is go home."

"I'm sure you'll be home soon enough."

Chapter 16

The Very Next Night

"Well, Mrs. Smith, you were wrong and I was right," Detective Kelly said as he sat in the living room at Elsa-May and Ettie's house along with retired detective Crowley.

"About Nora George?"

"Yes."

"It seems so." Ettie frowned, disappointed that she'd been wrong at first about Nora.

"She was so convincing," Elsa-May said.

"That's true, she was. I even thought her husband was guilty at one point," Detective Kelly said.

"The only thing he was guilty of was being a liar and a cheat," Elsa-May said.

Crowley asked, "And the car that was seen all the time at Paula's house?"

"Paula admits that Cameron George visited her, but only to see if she was okay. They weren't carrying on an affair," Ettie explained. "And

Paula's brother has a similar car."

"But, Nora had followed her husband there and wouldn't have known the purpose of his visits," Kelly explained

"What did Nora think was happening when she got to the hospital and no guard was on the door?" Crowley asked.

"She would've thought, once her husband was arrested, that they thought they didn't need the police officer on her hospital door," Kelly said.

"Where would she have gotten that insulin from?" Elsa-May asked. "You can't get that over the counter at a pharmacy, can you?"

"No. Casey Campbell is a diabetic. She confessed that she gave the insulin to Nora and she also gave us a full confession of her part in the attack on Paula."

"Will she be charged with murder as well?" Ettie asked.

"Casey will most likely be charged for conspiracy to commit murder and for obstruction of justice. She might not get as long a sentence as Nora, but she'll get a pretty long time I'd suspect."

"We were right about Obadiah Lapp not being guilty," Elsa-May said.

"Yes, you were," Crowley said.

"I'm just thankful that Paula pulled through without any ill effects."

"It's a miracle, and that's what the doctor told me," Detective Kelly said.

"Well, we believe in those," Ettie said.

Elsa-May pushed herself to her feet. "Anyone for coffee and cake?"

"Always," Detective Kelly said.

"I won't say no," Crowley answered.

While Elsa-May headed to the kitchen, Ettie asked the detectives, "Is this the strangest case you've ever worked? I thought it was Cameron and then at one point I thought it was Casey. I never guessed until the last that it was Nora, and having Casey helping her made it even more confusing."

"It was a mystery, that's for certain," Kelly said.

"Ettie, how did you figure out that Casey was involved?"

"It was when I heard that she'd come forward to say that Cameron did it, and it kept playing on my mind that the taxi driver delivered a woman to the street that night and dropped her up the road and not at a particular house. There's nothing else in that area except houses. I got to thinking what a perfect plan for Nora to have, and to make it work, the cherry on top was for Casey to come forward and say Cameron confessed it to her."

"And no one would've thought that Nora and Casey would've known one another well enough to plot a crime so horrendous," Kelly said.

"At one point I thought that Nora George and Paula's brother might have had some dealings, but I guess that didn't make much sense," Crowley said.

Elsa-May brought a tray of coffee and cake out, placing it on the coffee table in the center of the room. "Nothing about the whole thing made sense. I'm just glad it's finally over and there's a happy ending. Paula's healthy and safe."

"Nora and Casey teamed together against a common enemy—Cameron George, who was being unfaithful to both of them," Ettie said. "Paula is going to move back in with the Lapps for a few weeks when she gets out of the hospital, which has made Obadiah quite happy." Ettie giggled.

Kelly said, "That's a good idea. She'll have someone close by to look after her until she gets back on her feet."

"Exactly," Elsa-May said. "Ettie and I will be sure to keep an eye on her as well."

"All's well that ends well," Kelly said as he took the piece of cake that Elsa-May offered him.

"Thanks to both of you," Detective Kelly said nodding to Elsa-May and Ettie.

"I told you that these ladies would be helpful to you," Crowley said.

Kelly laughed.

"Have a piece of cake," Elsa-May said holding the cake plate in front of him.

"What's funny?" Ettie asked as Kelly took a slice of cake.

He shook his head. "I'm laughing because we never agree on anything, but everything always turns out well in the end."

"It was just as well that Paula woke up when she did, then. Would you have believed my theory if she hadn't?" Ettie asked.

"Of course, I would've, Ettie, of course," Detective Kelly said before he took a large mouthful of cake.

Thank you for your interest in

Betrayed

Ettie Smith Amish Mysteries Book 7

* * * * * * * * * * * * *

For updates on
Samantha Price's new releases
subscribe to her newsletter at:
http://www.samanthapriceauthor.com

Other books in this series:

Ettie Smith Amish Mysteries Book 1

<u>Secrets Come Home</u>

After Ettie Smith's friend, Agatha, dies, Ettie is surprised to find that Agatha has left her a house. During building repairs, the body of an Amish man who disappeared forty years earlier is discovered under the floorboards.

When it comes to light that Agatha and the deceased man were once engaged to marry, the police declare Agatha as the murderer.

Ettie sets out to prove otherwise.

Soon Ettie hears rumors of stolen diamonds, rival criminal gangs, and a supposed witness to the true murderer's confession.

When Ettie discovers a key, she is certain it holds the answers she is looking for.

Will the detective listen to Ettie's theories when he sees that the key belongs to a safe deposit box?

Ettie Smith Amish Mysteries Book 2
<u>Amish Murder</u>

When a former Amish woman, Camille Esh, is murdered, the new detective in town is frustrated that no one in the Amish community will speak to him. The detective reluctantly turns to Ettie Smith for help. Soon after Ettie agrees to see what she can find out, the dead woman's brother, Jacob, is arrested for the murder. To prove Jacob's innocence, Ettie delves into the mysterious and secretive life of Camille Esh, and uncovers one secret after another.

Will Ettie be able to find proof that Jacob is innocent, even though the police have DNA evidence against him, and documentation that proves he's guilty?

Can Ettie uncover the real murderer amongst the many people who had reasons to want Camille dead?

Ettie Smith Amish Mysteries Book 3:
<u>Murder in the Amish Bakery</u>

When Ettie has problems with her bread sinking in the middle, she turns to her friend, Ruth Fuller, who owns the largest Bakery in town.

When Ruth and Ettie discover a dead man in Ruth's Bakery with a knife in his back, Ruth is convinced the man was out to steal her bread recipe.

It was known that the victim, Alan Avery, was one of the three men who were desperate to get their hands on Ruth's bread secrets.

When it's revealed that Avery owed money all over town, the local detective believes he was after the large amount of cash that Ruth banks weekly.

Why was Alan Avery found with a Bible clutched in his hand? And what did it have to do with a man who was pushed down a ravine twenty years earlier?

Ettie Smith Amish Mysteries Book 4
<u>Amish Murder Too Close</u>

Elderly Amish woman, Ettie Smith, finds a body outside her house. Everything Ettie thought she knew about the victim is turned upside down when she learns the dead woman was living a secret life. As the dead woman had been wearing an engagement ring worth close to a million dollars, the police must figure out whether this was a robbery gone wrong. When an Amish man falls under suspicion, Ettie has no choice but to find the real killer.

What information about the victim is Detective Kelly keeping from Ettie?

When every suspect appears to have a solid alibi, will Ettie be able to find out who murdered the woman, or will the Amish man be charged over the murder?

Book 5
Amish Quilt Shop Mystery

Amish woman, Bethany Parker, finally realizes her dream of opening her own quilt shop. Yet only days after the grand opening, when she invites Ettie Smith to see her store, they discover the body of a murdered man.

At first Bethany is concerned that the man is strangely familiar to her, but soon she has more pressing worries when she discovers her life is in danger.

Bethany had always been able to rely on her friend, Jabez, but what are his true intentions toward her?

Book 6
Amish Baby Mystery

Ettie and her sister, Elsa-May, find an abandoned baby boy wrapped in an Amish quilt on their doorstep. Ettie searches for clues as to the baby's identity and finds a letter in the folds of the quilt. The letter warns that if they don't keep the baby hidden, his life will be in danger.

When the retired Detective Crowley stumbles onto their secret, they know they need to find the baby's mother fast.

Will Ettie and Elsa-May be able to keep the baby safe and reunite him with his parents before it's too late?

What does the baby have to do with a cold case kidnapping that happened years before?

Samantha Price loves to hear from her readers.
Connect with Samantha at:
samanthaprice333@gmail.com
http://twitter.com/AmishRomance
http://www.facebook.com/SamanthaPriceAuthor

89355367R00108

Made in the USA
Lexington, KY
27 May 2018